THE DOOR BETWEEN US

THE DARKEST SEA

THE DOOR BETWEEN US

ANNA.M.L

Published by

THE DARKEST SEA

www.thedarkestsea.com

Copyright © 2016, 2023 ANNA.M.L

ISBN paperback: 978-0-6456741-2-5

ISBN e-book: 978-0-6456741-3-2

First published 2023

Cover design by ANNA.M.L

For the children of the dark

PREFACE

In going from room to room in the dark,

I reached out blindly to save my face,

But neglected, however lightly, to lace

My fingers and close my arms in an arc.

A slim door got in past my guard,

And hit me a blow in the head so hard

I had my native simile jarred.

So people and things don't pair anymore

With what they used to pair with before.

- *The Door in the Dark, Robert Frost*[1]

[1] Frost, Robert. "The Door in the Dark" from *West Runing Brook*. First edition 1928 Henry Holt & Co.

CHAPTER ONE

Damien hid to the side behind the trestle vine, out of view from the driveway. He didn't want her to see him waiting. He was used to waiting now. And he was sick of waiting inside. The house was small and there were too many places that left him exposed. Today he would rather be outside in the biting cold than be caught inside.

It had been four weeks since his mother Cynthia had come home. He had seen her rather sporadically off and on in the weeks prior. He remembered she had a little bundle firmly clutched in her arms - his baby brother Rory. In the hospital they had let him hold the baby briefly in his arms. He found him an odd little creature all shrunken and red and couldn't open his marble eyes properly. He had wanted to stay that day, because he didn't know what had happened to her, his mother. She had gone away and once he found her again, in the hospital, he didn't understand why his grandmother Claudia had firmly insisted he come back home, that Cynthia needed her rest. Four weeks ago she had come home, then went. He didn't know where.

Two weeks ago his grandmother had said she was coming

home. She had dressed him in a new shirt and polished his shoes, and as he sat there on the sofa in the living room waiting in earnest, he heard his grandpa, Frank, walk in the front door saying she couldn't come. His grandmother had peered into the living room and when their faces met, he quietly stood up from the sofa and walked to his bedroom. He didn't want to be caught like that again, he knew what his grandmother had seen in his face, the way she had reflected it back at him.

Today all he could hope for was that she would turn up, and that she might stay longer than the two hours she stayed last time. She had been fussing over the baby, never letting him go and he felt like he was the visitor quietly sitting back staying out of the way. Today Claudia was busying herself preparing sandwiches in the kitchen.

He could hear his grandfather's truck coming up the long driveway. Its heavy grit rankled his ears. The closer it came to the house, his heart leapt with frightened anticipation, swiftly followed by a sinking feeling. As the truck came to a stop on the gravel, he peered through the vines down low, keeping out of view. He could feel the cold damp air through the wool of his sweater. There he saw his mother's delicate legs step out of the truck onto the ground like a demoiselle crane descending. A cataclysmic crunch of emotions wrung him, throttling him round to the back of the house where he pretended to play in the back garden, protected by the clusters of juniper bushes, shaded by the Norwegian Sunsets dark from morning rain.

"Damien" a voice called from the back door. "Come and see who is home." Damien timidly made his way to the back door and walked into the house.

"Hello my darling," Cynthia greeted as she splayed her arms out motioning Damien to her. His grandmother held Rory, swaying him in gentle motions with a smile on her face.

Damien coyly walked up to his mother and she leaned forward to give him a peck on the cheek. She looked different to him. She looked white, like she hadn't been outside in the sun for a while. There was a stiffness in the way she had greeted him, not the same as how she used to be, her face seemed drawn, tired. Nevertheless, she was here, that's all that mattered. And that was her suitcase sitting on the floor in the hallway like a stump of a tree that should have always been there.

The days turned into weeks, turned into months. And she was still there, but she wasn't there at all. Seasons opened and closed like a leather-bound book with unread contents. Damien would walk passed her sitting in the living room, staring listlessly out the window into the front garden. She was disconnected. Sometimes he saw her walking around the house looking lost, which he didn't understand how, because the house was so small. The living room lamp with its hourglass china was a stronger womanly presence. In these times, he wanted his father. He would run to his bedroom and pull out the keyboard his father had given him as a gift. Pinging on the keys produced a sound like honey, reminding him of who gave it to him and of that day when his mother hugged him with a smile on her face as she helped him blow out his candles. She was soft like cotton candy. The reminder created a warmness that was a safer haven away from the cold room in which his mother was starting to permanently inhabit.

Then she disappeared again, Rory along with her.

CHAPTER TWO

She wasn't there. He knew. But he couldn't help a furtive look into the room his mother had been sleeping in. Before he reached his own room each night he peered in, in some hope maybe she had suddenly appeared and returned to it and he would make out her form lying on the bed in the dark. Even after weeks had passed, he couldn't stop the habit, until one night his eyes had played tricks on him and he was sure he saw someone in the room. So convinced, he raced into the recessed darkness with heart pounding to launch onto a bed that was flat and cold and devoid of any life form. From then on, he trained himself not to look.

While his eyes played tricks they also started to perceive looks. The look of worry in his grandmother's face and the look of awkward compassion in his grandfather's and forced smiles hiding something behind them. And he had started to collect the catchphrases - "it can't be helped"; "it's ok"; "it's for the best"; "everything will be fine"; "it'll be alright"; "we'll look after you." But they had started to become as common as mud and as comparably dirty. Dirty words that he didn't understand their meaning, never followed through with a proper explanation. Just hanging in the air. That along with the lady in church who gave him an obscure stare only made him want to run.

Every afternoon he ran into the yard away from the people and the words that made no sense out into an adjacent field, skirting its perimeter. It was cordoned off with a wood and wire fence, an incompatible Green Gables[2]. He'd find a stick and drag it over the ground along the line of the fence following its dips and crevices, unconsciously tracing its line back home despite his infinite desire to get lost. Old bits of metal, nails and screws gradually made their way into his pocket.

He'd walked this hackneyed path too many times, it needed his own design. He had commenced building a mini fortress along one of the fence posts after collecting bits of wood and rock over the last few days. It was far enough from the path that nothing would come near it to threaten its destruction. His fingers dug into the dirt to scrape up the earth and create a mound and a moat around the base. Splintered pieces of wood from an old paling, snapped off like brittle bones were stuck into the mound as a piling platform before rocks were shoved between them to solidify the base. He ripped off the loose hanging bark at the base of the trunk of a paperbark tree. It ripped like a stringy masking tape losing its tack. It was the perfect shroud for a wall around the outside and a soft floor inside. Twigs jammed into the crevices of the fence post above creating a spikey crown for its roof.

He sat back resting on his knees, proud of the structure he created.

"That's good," he said out loud. He pulled out the screws and nails from his pocket and placed them inside like little

---

[2]Montgomery, L. M. *Anne of Green Gables.* 1908 L.C. Page & Co.

soldiers, lined up in their metal armour. He jigged them along the floor striking between them in mock clashes spraying them all asunder in the mini rotunda before lining them all up again like a row of pawns in a chess game.

Metal was something tangible and hard to the touch, firmer than any grip of a human on him. The scent of its steel grubbier by the earth upon his fingers, rendered a sense of strength thwarting the invading weeks without anyone touching him at all. Metal was masculine. With the size of an inch it was within his control. He liked this game of play.

As the air started to nip and the sun started to set, he collected the toy soldier screws and nails and put them back in his pocket to take back to the house, where he emptied them into a container on the veranda, tucked in a corner hidden behind the flowers of the tangled clematis. He took his shoes off at the back door. Claudia had roused on him for walking dirt through the house and as he looked down he was covered in it. He brushed off as much as he could which was mostly on the knees of his trousers until they were clear of any debris, then opened the back door.

"Dinner time Damien," she called as she heard the scuff of his shoes in the hall. He stood to attention at her gentle command and trailed his way to the dining room.

The plates were carefully placed one by one for the three of them, surrounding the ornamental paper flowers that were carefully arranged in a tiny vase in the centre. Claudia gently walked into the room with two crockery pots before swinging back to collect another. The cross hatched gingham of her apron matched the serviettes. Frank walked in with a scent of men-shed familiarity and Claudia's delicate breeze back to the table brought the gravy.

Damien squinted his eyes as he blessed the Lord for these thy gifts. At its bounty he comfortably closed his eyes. The salty mush of his grandmother's stew mixed in with the wet cornmeal was delectable. He remembered the last thing his mother made were lamb chops with potato mash and ketchup, which he hoped she would make for him again when she was back. He was sure she would be back, because she knew he liked them. He hadn't the heart to ask when she would be back, relenting instead to awkward silence, meal after meal, sure that he would be informed when the time was right. Something about "training for a job" was mentioned to him at one point by his grandmother, a concept of which he did not understand how it would impinge on contact and create removal. He hid the thought with downcast eyes until he looked back up at the indifference the two of them carried in their own. An ease he tried to comprehend that he couldn't somehow feel. All comprehension of the world he inhabited changed the day he learned his father had died. Everything stopped. Including conversation of him.

"I noticed a broken branch on the Elm by the front fence." Claudia quietly announced.

"It could topple the post."

"Yes, well, you might want to ask Jim to come and take a look before it falls on the fence."

"I'll head in to Sullivan's tomorrow." Frank assured with calm authority.

The runs into the adjacent town were the highlight of any day in the week, especially if Frank took Damien and let him swing past where his father used to work. It was a tangible place where he could at least check whether his father still existed. The unknown abode of his mother was thwarted by the surety of place of his father. The only *known* place, however, was the one of his mind where he would pair the two of them together again. He jostled between the images he remembered of when he had last seen them standing side by side – a picture that was starting to diminish the more he pressed on with it. Instead he pressed the gingham serviette against his lips.

"Remind him about the mains roots. He still owes us for that one."

"He'll do right by us, don't worry about that." Frank assured.

"Hmm, that's what *he* said last time and we had to wait three months for him to return."

"Yes, yes." Frank downplayed.

She stood up from the table collecting the empty plates. "Yes, yes, I hope you follow through." She reflected, unable to resist a subtle nag from years of skilfully quiet persistence, then dashed a smile at Damien.

Damien helped his grandmother clear the plates, passing them up to her as she rinsed them under the sink, stacked and ready for washing. She turned to him declaring to wash him first. He dawdled his way behind her following the back knot of her apron into the bathroom, where the plug in the hole and the squeak of the hot and cold pins poured out the reminder that the day was now closed, like the inevitable fall from a high. She pulled off his clothes and he stepped into the tub. The water quickly became a murky hue the moment he washed away the day's residue from the field still clinging to his skin in secret.

"Any news?" Claudia inquired as she washed him down with Ivory® soap.

He knew to what she was referring. His mother's phone call. That afternoon she had called and he had asked her where she was. "In school like you," she had said down the line. Her response had just confused him more – because he hadn't seen her there at all. He decided not to pursue any further line of inquiry on it for looking like a fool. He just repeated back to Claudia what he'd been told. A shameful ignorance sank in his gut like the drop of the Ivory bar to the bottom of the tub. The phone call had been too short for him to ask her anything more.

Claudia tipped the bucket of water over his head. The warming cascade over his shoulders was like a brush against familiar skin, before the biting cold of the room slapped him, reminding him bath time was only ever a quick exercise in which he could never overstay its welcome. She wrapped him in the blue towel she bought especially for him. But it was his bed that hugged him with arms of want. With the covers up, he snuggled in between the sheets, nuzzling his head in the pillow as deep as it would go, disappearing. A sense of collapsing and folding dug as deep as the earth he had been trying to dig, too young to understand the concept of sleep that came so easily the moment he closed his eyes.

CHAPTER THREE

She was a tall woman, solidly built with a demeanour as stern as her firmly fitting blouse. Mrs Fletcher's physical presence shaped a demonic figure to any God-fearing child in the classroom, but in some strange twist of perceptions, she had a soft spot for Damien that both scared as much as it placated him. Mumbles dispersed through the space as echoes spliced by the confident swerve of chalk on blackboard, as she demonstrated, and they answered her questions. Damien's ears pricked up and his heart skipped a beat any time he heard his name emerge from her jaw.

"The next one, Mr Zane?" She called to Damien with her back to him, as she remained poised awaiting a response. He stared at the board emblazoned with the chalk of 4 x 4.

"Come on you know this one," she said curtly looking at him directly, then back to the board.

"Sixteen." He said.

"That's the way." She commended with firm assurance.

Damien turned to his friend Patrick in the next seat and made a 'don't look at me' face. Patrick was a lanky boy with Irish ears and a pale face that seemed to be a good complement to his friend's wiry pocket size frame and cocoa black hair. They were both quiet boys who seemed perfectly in tune with one another, who both knew how to sit quietly and pay attention in class and equally how to escape unnoticed in the playground disappearing from view. Damien had discovered he was good at arithmetic and Patrick a humble concomitant. Mrs Fletcher, upon this discovery often tack-toed between the two of them testing their knowledge or otherwise relying in hope on an answer that would be correct from what was a small class of the first-grade. Once they had learned how to add, now on approach to the end of the year, they had started to multiply. Frank had stuck a multiplication table on the wall in his bedroom upon which he would consult prior to the leftfield quiz that had started to spring up at the dinner table. It was a test for which he never expected that made him permanently ensconced in the wall-tacked oracle. He didn't want to get it wrong. In class it only aided and abetted in his favour.

At lunch they only ate the insides of their sandwiches, after picking through peanut butter with the crusts cut off, discarding the slices of bread. Of more interest was to run down the back of the emerald paddock and re-enact battle scenes and chase one another until they tired, covered in scratches and grass stains, a product of enough tag and snatch moments propagating their tumbles.

Damien swung out his arms and made for its kamikaze into Patrick's body.

"Kapuschhhh."

"Aahh!" Patrick guffawed with faux pain before pushing him off.

"Thshu! Thshu!" Damien thrust through his teeth.

"Pow! Pow!" Patrick returned fire.

"You're meant to lie down now."

"Says who?"

"I got you first."

"No you didn't."

"Yes I did."

"You crashed."

"Yeah, *I* crashed into *you*."

Back in the classroom, they returned to obedience as though an open switch blade had slunk them from their exterior selves back into form. They listened attentively with nervous curiosity completing each exercise presented to them. To Damien, it all made sense. It was easy. After finishing exercises ahead of everyone else, he sat alert to his teacher's possible gaze while noticing all the little details inhabiting her desk at the front of the room, whether she had an apple sitting on it, what colour it was, the number of coloured pencils in a canister and how many books lay beside it.

Of dominance was the hand cranked planetary sharpener hooked to the side of her desk, which she invited the students up one by one at the end of the day to sharpen their pencils ahead of the next day's class. There was something acutely deceptive to Damien in the tactile feel of a wooden pencil disappearing into the metal vice. The stick like protrusion stuck from a small black hole subtly vibrating and churning in his hand with each spin, scraping the tip of the pencil to a spike brought great satisfaction. He was its engineer. He had perfect control over the sharpness of its tip. He liked his pencils sharp. He was mystified at what went on inside that black hole and would try and peer inside when no-one was looking. He had a curiosity for the dark places of the unseeable. After he had scraped like a curette he returned to his desk and neatly line his lead pencils and eraser along the top. There was routine, a familiarity in this exercise that was a comfort and acknowledged the return of the next day, one where he would be prepared. He liked to know that everything would be in its place, as it should be, arranged.

Leaving class for the pick-up by his grandpa Frank was the vanilla sponge of the afternoon. Damien cherished the truck. Frank was a quiet man and never said much, just enough which leant a safe comfort as he sat in the front, his head just visible over the line of the wind screen as they trundled through the streets on the way home. He'd trace the line of the overhead wires from pole to pole, their black liquorice stringing him along to home, sweetening the journey with a backdrop of maples. It was predictable, and he knew where it led.

Until where it led started to become unpredictable when reality dawned its unpalatable metal. Metal was cool on the tongue. When the truck turned into the driveway of his grandparents' home, a quivering sensation had started to subtly overwhelm him and persist, spreading over his body. It creeped as the weeks went by to the point of its noticeability. He didn't know what it was. He just knew it as '*it*'. There was something about entering the drive on approach to the house. The in-between. Once inside, the feeling subsided. He'd thought it was the chill in the cab of the truck and had started to pack an extra sweater for the drive home. But it didn't seem to matter. Whether it was the known safety of the four walls around him or the sound of Claudia somewhere rustling in the house that placated him, he didn't know.

One afternoon she was out, and the creeping feeling didn't leave him. He sat in the stillness of the living room. The air was so still, he could see the slithers of dust aloft in the stream of sun from the window. The scent of the dust upon the furniture was acute in his nostrils. It heightened the room's uninhabitable status with abundance. He ran to his bedroom, sure of its solace, where usually the feeling would go when he could hear Claudia come home. Claudia's footsteps through the front door were the medicinal quell.

The recompense of an afternoon phone call from his mother started to do little to alleviate the disquiet humming through his being. The striking sound of a ringing phone was a failed placebo. A phone call alleviated the fear she may have been dead, but the breaks between them and their repetition reinforced she was somewhere else – a place he didn't know, with his words lost down the line to her. A ringing phone was loud and it pierced with a shocking sting that made his heart flutter like a butterfly confused, in an excitement before a shattering crunch. The contractions of the muscle of his heart crushed it knowing there was no follow through after the conversation closed. Its repetition rendered its fact.

If he could leap through those afternoons and make it to bed, it was the only place *it* went altogether. For today, at least, Claudia was home.

She poured him a glass of milk and gave him a cookie. An old wood stove was in the kitchen and with its stoking made it the warmest part of the house. He sat at the kitchen table and watched her pull out vegetables washing them under water in the sink. She was a trim, petite woman, quiet and no-nonsense. He was used to, for a small time, seeing two female bodies inhabit this space. Now there was only one. Today she started to peel potatoes.

"Go on. Run outside," she ushered to him. The rest of the house was quiet and cold. So if Claudia didn't want him watching her in the kitchen, outside wasn't going to be any worse. He stepped out the back door and the sharpness of the spring air in the late afternoon still had a certain bite.

He liked to go down to the creek, which was a few fields passed the house. He knew he would be able to make it there and back before the day fell black. But his grandmother didn't like him wandering down there by himself. Damien decided to take a different route instead via an adjacent field that led to a small brook that trickled from the mouth of the creek. It wasn't far from the back of the house so was easy to find his way back.

He slashed at the overgrown grasses with his arms as he traipsed through the field toward a towering row of pine trees. As he entered the cluster of trees and skirted down the cracked bank, it blocked out the afternoon sky behind him. The opposite bank inclined up a steep hill lush with fern saplings, ivy and wooded undergrowth. The coolness springing from the stream of water freshened the air and impeccably bounced off the aroma of pine needles from their canopy above like a cave with a roof of moss.

"It's OK. It's best." He picked up a stone on the bank and skimmed it across the water aiming downstream. "You don't have to worry."

It was here he found a place where he could talk out loud. He'd repeat conversations he overheard and recite words spoken to him. Trying to understand, then convince himself of their meaning. He would rephrase all the words he thought he had spoken to them, unsure they had heard him properly, sure he had said them right.

"Mrs Fletcher liked me today. She said I did a good job."

He skirted along the bank, crunching on the muddied earth and crushed slate and picked up a crooked stick, half poking out of the water. He could see down through the clear water where there was a small tadpole darting between rocks. He started to poke the stick around in the tadpole's swimming pool.

"What are you doing?" a girl's voice gently beckoned behind him.

Without surprise and showing no restraint he obliged in

a response to her, still staring at the water. "It's a tadpole. He's stuck. Can't get out."

"Where is he meant to go?"

"Well, if I can get him out of this section here, he can make his way downstream."

"Where will that get him?"

"To the river," Damien replied matter of fact.

"Why can't he stay here?" the girl pressed.

"Because that is where he is meant to go." He quipped in a 'don't you know anything' tone. He looked up at her for the first time. She was a wisp of a girl with long brown hair and a splash of freckles scattered across her round nose. She looked about the same age as him and continued to peer inquisitively over his shoulder.

"I'm Ava," she said.

Damien turned back to the water and continued his efforts to free the tadpole, by swirling the water hole creating an eddying flow. The light started to fade like a globe in decline and it was harder to see into the water.

"Well, I might have to try again tomorrow," he concluded. He stood up from the bank and turned toward the break in the trees leading back to the field behind him.

Ava turned to him. "Where are you going?"

"I had better go back, my grandma doesn't like me to be outside after dark. And there's snakes."

"Maybe tomorrow then." She wistfully intoned.

Ava leaned down to pick up a small stone at her feet. She crouched down and skimmed it across the water, instead it ricocheted off another rock.

"That's not how you do it," he remarked.

Damien turned back and made his way out into the field to make it back before nightfall, before the air got keen. The trail back in the dark made him aware he was the only one who could get himself home. Made him aware he was alone. Made him aware of the night.

This night he didn't so much mind. With the night there was going to be a tomorrow. Tomorrow was when he could try again. Tonight was a good night because tomorrow was going to be a good day. Frank had promised to take him to the store.

Back in his room he sorted through his comic books. Three of them should be enough to take with him, together with the matchbox car his father had given him the last time he saw him. He bundled them together into his back pack and rested it by the door. Claudia had neatly pressed his favourite t-shirt where it gently rested on a hanger on the knob in humble wait for its adorner.

CHAPTER FOUR

The counter was long and wide like a cargo container and the perfect place to hide and sit and wait. There was something homely about it as he sat on the floor, like a smell of his father's leather shoes at the bottom of a closet. Damien delicately fingered through his comics while Frank was with the cashier. Frank brought Damien into the town's electronic store from time to time when he needed to pick something up. His father's home had been a few blocks from the store.

Damien didn't really comprehend what it was his father did, he just knew that the electronics store was a place stacked with little gadgets, televisions and the source of the keyboard that had been the gift from him. As perplexed and dazzled by all the contraptions it housed, the delight was that it was where his father had been and that he had waited with him once beside the counter. He would have been happy to stay there all day than go back home to his grandparents. And so many times he was on the verge of asking that very question – could he stay, but he never knew how to form the words that would ask it the right way. Because he had tried and failed. Even as young as he was he had started to formulate and pre-empt that it wasn't permitted to ask such questions. Adults seemed to like to speak for him and would put words into his mouth before he dare utter them. There had been too many attempts. It stifled and bubbled within him and often made him stuck and confused what he should do. So he usually did nothing, but stare through the haze building in front of them.

Frank was now the stalwart to the son of another man, with consideration derived from searching for a sense of ease in an uneasy situation. His mother found it hard to make ends meet and keeping Damien was an option for which she had to deny. The elders seemed to rule in favour of what was best and made the call on behalf of their adult children, that's what he told himself anyway.

It was Saturday and a friend of his mother's had promised to take him to the Showground where they ran the fair. Damien had brought along with him the five dollars that he had saved from the fifty cents he had started to receive each week. It was enough to buy some sweets and pay for a couple of rides, but John made him put away his cash and paid for everything he wanted.

"Do you want to have a go?" John gestured toward a parlour game as they walked through the alley. Damien nodded. It involved throwing golf sized balls into a moving conveyer belt of cups, the trick was to get the ball in the cup that had a blue duck behind it. He walked up to the platform and grabbed a ball from the box. He threw it overarm too hard and it smashed and bounced off the wooden panelling.

"Oh!" he scowled.

"Ooh," John crooned. "Do another one. Try it underarm."

"Damien took another ball and swung it underarm a little more softly. It just tipped the edge of a cup but missed.

"Argh." Damien grimaced under his breath.

"One more. Go for the one with the duck."

Damien picked up one last ball and swung it under arm again and it knocked the cup and the duck over entirely off the belt. No wonder they painted those ducks blue like a bruise.

"Almost!" John exclaimed. Damien looked to John not sure what it meant.

"Did I win anything?" He asked curiously.

"Not quite, it has to be in the cup. Never mind. You can have a go next time."

Families walked passed enjoying the early evening festivities and others sat at tables near the food vans. The saltiness in the air wrung an insatiability that dug at their stomachs and revealed the plying of the way to a young man's heart. John bought hotdogs and Cokes® and they sat at a picnic table quietly eating, just the two of them, unconscious to the ordinariness of those who stained its planks weathered by the years before them.

"So how has school been?"

"It's ok." Damien let out through a half munch of food.

"Any new friends?"

"Just Patrick." He contained.

"Should bring him along next time."

"Maybe." Damien sagely replied. He immediately rendered it null and void, not wanting anyone else to intersperse themselves in a space to be confined for him only.

"Hey there John," a middle-aged man stopped by as they ate.

"Hi Bobbie, good to see you."

"Ah, this must be your boy." The man looked at Damien with a friendly smile.

"A friend's."

Damien smiled shyly nodding.

"Well don't let me stop you." The man gestured a wave

and turned to walk on.

It was in this moment Damien was almost oblivious to everyone else around. Sitting in front of him was a man in the shape of a father. And he very rarely ate dinner with anyone other than his grandparents. For nearly a year he had been without that constant. That constant being either the man sitting in front of him or the mother he wasn't sure was ever returning. He resolved to eat his food as slowly as a puffing billy coming into its platform, hoping it never arrived to its end. The red skin wrapped mince in a soft floury bun was an effigy to harmony all housed within his belly.

"Well, better get you back." John checked his watch. "Have you had enough?"

Damien knocked his head side to side, shrugging his shoulders. It was never going to be enough, but he didn't know how to say no.

On the way back to the car John bought him a sachet of popping candy fizz. When he got in the front seat, he ripped the packet open and poured its contents into his mouth, squinting his eyes at the citric acid pop and crackle, its tang sizzling at the back of his tongue. It was the perfect distraction as the ignition of the car burned its way through his ears. He tried to see if there were any contents left to empty from the packet. John peered down at him, the showground lights illuminating the distance like a stagnant moon radiating out a too hot reflection of the sun. Seconds passed that felt like minutes. He gave in to an impulse.

"Hey," he said softly. Damien looked up. "Would you like to see my new place?"

Damien hunched out his chin "ok."

The apartment, with its mini kitchenette in the corner and a bathroom to the side was small and unglamorous. There was a bed at one end and a small brown sofa against a papered wall, where its embossed pattern reflected the paisley of a curling fern frond. These were all the details revealed as he opened the door letting Damien walk inside.

"Take a look around." He gently enthused before disappearing into the bathroom allowing Damien his own time to drink in the space.

As he stepped further into the room he closely surveyed the surroundings. He took it all in, the angles, the measurements, and the space. He turned back behind him, then forward and around and wandered over to sit on the sofa. He was convinced, he was certain, he knew for sure he would be able to fit in the corner up the back of the room. He was small and he knew he could fit there if only John could see it. Why couldn't he see that he could also fit in this room? Why hadn't he shown him this before when he could have worked this out?

John came out of the bathroom. Damien looked up in fervent hope.

"So how do you like my place?" He asked, trying to sound excited.

"It's good." Damien answered. His eyes beamed. His lips pinched.

"I know it's a bit small, but..." John trailed. Damien waited in hope for the sincerest of replies. "Well, I just wanted to show you where I was living since I moved from the end of your street."

An awkward silence dug between them.

"Well, I had better get you back so that Claudia knows where you are."

Damien's heart sank as though all the colourful balloons at the fair had shrunken in on themselves into a collapsed dark mass. It followed with his usual nod of agreeance. He would have rather not seen it than been given a taste of the place with his eyes. Rather than stand up from the sofa he didn't move a bone in his small body. He sat still.

"Can I stay here?" He asked knowing with the intellect he had that the space was too small. John gently halted, not expecting such a request.

"I'd have you here in a second," he stumbled, "but you get to have your own bedroom at your grandma's and she can make you proper dinners every night."

Damien looked down to the floor. The abyss of the wrong answer. The air suddenly felt hot as he breathed it in. As he breathed it out it fire-licked his cheeks. He could sense John shift. Then he asked the question he had wanted to ask for weeks.

"Do you know when my mummy is coming home?" He quietly snuck the words out of his mouth feeling the forbidden nature of them. He knew John knew his mother. Maybe he housed answers that never came from those always with him.

John took a deep breath and quietly let it out. He sat down on the seat beside him and rested his hand on Damien's tiny frame.

"Don't think about it."

This was not the heartfelt reassurance he wanted. He wasn't sure he would be convinced of its deflection, sure she would indeed materialise. John had delivered it disregarding his own words, hoping that the mother of a boy wouldn't give up on a life she seemingly only temporarily had to abandon to stand on her own two feet. Small towns did that to people. You had to leave in order to be able to stay. Anyhow, their whispers were a glue in the ear delivered by a pressure gun that Damien was starting to comprehend and no longer wanted to hear.

"We go?" John piped up in the awkward air.

Damien nodded his head, obligingly as he always had.

It was like a magnetic repulsion walking up the path in the dark toward the front door of home, leaking its glow-like syrup. Its nectar called for retreat fearing its tack would stick him in, unable to extract and head back to the place he would rather be. Frank was waiting in the doorway. He could hear the car behind him turn around and drive off. Something within him pulled away and out of his body, following invisible tail lights. He had turned away so he couldn't see them leave. As he walked into the house, Claudia walked in from the living room in her dressing gown and slippers, hair wrapped in rollers and a scarf.

"Come on young man, we had better get you ready for bed."

Damien walked into the bathroom and Claudia turned on the bath and pulled off his sweater and t-shirt. He undid the button of his shorts and pulled them down.

"In you get."

As water filled the tub he dipped his toes into its lukewarm. The warm sensation was at first distinct to his feet, then his legs and body like an amphibious creature finding its home of origin. But his shoulders felt cold. He felt strange. Like something was not quite right. The sound of his grandmother's chatter drowned out, sounding like a record wound backwards too slow. As she handed him a bar of soap she was asking him questions but he wasn't sure if his mouth was moving, if he was actually answering them. Minutes seemed lost until he was pulled up out of the bath and she was wrapping him in a towel drying him off. He could feel himself shiver.

He slipped into bed and the light was switched off, but the door was slightly ajar and light from the living room drifted in until it went out altogether. The house became quiet. He still felt odd. He wanted to get out of bed and run to his grandmother to tell her something was wrong. He pulled down the covers and swept out his feet. Sitting on the edge of the bed he stared into the dark shadowy room frantically searching for an exit. Black dots appeared along the wall and appeared to be getting bigger. Constricted and tight inside his chest, he couldn't move. Couldn't run. Couldn't get out. He wildly searched for a path to the door. He couldn't find it. He sucked in air that he couldn't breathe out until his cheeks became wet with tears.

CHAPTER FIVE

The sun streamed through the window shining a straw like colour through the dusty glass. A small jar which sat on the windowsill was full of marbles. The sun streaking it scattered a glimmering star like pattern on the wall beside the window. Damien reached for the jar and took the lid off. He gave a small sigh, looking about him, trying to figure out where else he could put them. He chanced upon a small brown box at the side of his wardrobe and proceeded to tip the marbles into it. They clanked noisily as he poured them into their new home. He anxiously looked up and around to check his grandparents weren't within earshot to query what he was doing.

Walking out the back door with the jar and through the field he continued down to the brook with a singular purpose. The days were getting warmer and the sky was blue azure overhead. When Damien walked down the embankment through the foliage and trees again it was like he was entering a different place. The blue-sky brightness was gone, but the warm air still lingered enough to suppress the water's coldness. The sun high and undisturbed by clouds, sparkled through the cracks and breaks in the trees, reflecting off the stream. It lit up the lichen slapped like petals upon the boulders that shouldered the curving stream where pebbles rested like strings of broken pearls along its inlets. Damien liked this little dark oasis. A scent of moist soil and damp foliage laced with citron was his private Eden. It was peaceful. It was quiet except for the sound of the gurgling waters, the amphibians and crickets.

He walked down the side of the bank back to the same spot as he had before to the place where he found the little pool between rocks. There he could see in the waters the tadpoles swimming about as he had before. He unscrewed the lid of the jar.

"You came back." A familiar voice could be heard. Ava was standing beside him like a welcome intrusion peering at the jar. "What are you doing?"

Damien looked up and addressed her with the adroitness of a young man skilled in the matter of science. "I just have to pick them up in this jar..." but before he could finish Ava's unresisting curiosity tumbled out.

"Why are you doing that for?"

"Because they are stuck here." Damien impatiently continued. "They can't get out of here while they are in there. So you have to help take them out."

"Hm." Ava mulled.

"If you don't they will die in there." Damien matter of fact put to her.

"How do you know where to take them though?"

"Well, my grandpa has taken me down to the main river. This feeds all the way down there. That's where all the frogs are. They need to be down there so they can turn into frogs."

Ava jumped up and twirled around on one of the boulders on the bank, her skirt puffed up like the cup of a bluebell.

"But how did they get here in the first place?" She queried.

Damien stopped to think of what the right answer was. He wasn't sure. She'd stumped him for a second, but then logic prevailed. He had been given picture books on the life of frogs and his mind started to madly scan what he had seen in them.

"The frogs come back up here from the river at night and they plant more tadpoles." Damien bent down and scooped the jar into the small pool trying to capture the frenetic specimens. Ava lay on her belly on the boulder staring down transfixed at Damien's carefully magical motion.

"Ooh, nearly," she winced as he had scooped the jar too quickly and they all swam out bouncing over the rim like the tips of squid ink noodles escaping the edges of a bubbling saucepan.

Damien tipped the jar deeper under water and as they entered the ring, he lifted it up slowly. Done. He screwed the lid back on the jar and held it up in admiration.

"See!" He said with a smile.

"Yes!" Ava returned.

Damien walked up away from the bank and Ava jumped up and followed, as he made his way through the scrub toward the field.

"I thought tadpoles turned into eels." She swayed.

Damien screwed up his face at her. "Eels come from snakes." Ava bobbed her head from side to side satisfied with his convincing command.

"So are you going to take them to the river now?" She skipped along beside him.

"I might have to take them tomorrow."

"Can I come?" She said with an air of enthusiasm, flicking her hair behind her.

"Well, maybe." Damien replied cautiously.

They skirted along the trail by the perimeter fence. The old fortress Damien had built was still intact along one of the posts. He stopped by it when he noticed one of the sticks had fallen, placing the jar on the brown earth, the tadpoles squirming around in their aquarium bowl. He picked up the stick and tried to correct it.

"Is this your castle?" Ava inquired.

"It's a fortress."

"It looks like a castle. Like at the beach."

Damien looked at her obtusely. "Castles don't have spikes. This is a fortress because it is spikey." Not that he knew what a castle on a beach looked like. He had never been to the beach.

Ava picked some dandelions that were protruding from the side of the fence and placed them at the corners of the moat at the base of Damien's fortress. She picked a couple of heads off the flowers and put them inside his temple.

"For their beds. They need something soft to lie on."

Damien didn't like that she was messing with his fortress, but he didn't want to tell her otherwise. He accepted her contribution and attention to detail and decided to keep moving. He picked up the jar and walked back towards the house, leaving Ava dallying in the soil.

Once he walked through the back door, Claudia was waiting for him, giving him a stern look. She had been paying for piano lessons for him for the last year, taking him into town in the afternoon once a week to Mrs White, who was teaching him.

"Come on Damien, you'll make yourself terribly late. Today's not the day for playing outside."

Damien scurried passed her taking his jar into his bedroom.

"Chop, chop," she motioned behind him. "Wash your hands and your face please. Can't have you a mess in front of Mrs White."

Damien dumped the jar on his bedside table, its life aquatic frenetically swishing around inside, then scooted into the bathroom hurriedly splashing water and soap on his face and between his hands.

"Where's your book?" Claudia softly queried.

"Here." Damien lunged to the piano in the living room, where his practice sheet music sat on top of the piano.

"Good, now come on, let's go." Claudia murmured, her handbag and keys at the ready, ushering Damien out the front door.

Piano lessons were another world for Damien. Another world with another adult telling him what to do, but one where he was slowly comfortably inhabiting, without the need to be told a thing. He liked to be able to play, to prove he could do what they told him to do. He liked Mrs White, but she was a stickler for detail, for perfectionism with each key he hit. She encouraged and enthused, demanded precision, but always with an air of praise. When he could play a piece without fault, he could see her elated response, and craved the things she would say when he played right. "They will be so proud of you," she would say. Who *they* were he wasn't sure – was there something she knew that he didn't? So he played with determination, wanting to believe what she told him, so he could show *them* himself. He wanted to prove her right as much as he wanted to prove it for himself. But the need to prove was somehow always jostling for position with the feeling it gave him, the sound it gave him, which was his alone that no-one could trespass. The way he could make a note ring out to portray what the empty space around him wanted to reveal of how he within that empty space felt. Mrs White taught him bars at a time and he could play it back frivolous and light, gregarious and sweet, or slumberous with a pervading quiver, just as she had displayed. He liked how he could strike one note hard and another soft and it pulsed out of him what his heart wanted if it had a nerve attaching to the end of his fingertips. And he was learning fast. Scales, arpeggios, basic allegros and simple pieces were like walking on a lily pad in a still pond.

"Now Damien, look closely at this one." Mrs White turned to him looking serious on the stool beside him. She pulled out some pages from a small pile of sheet music on top of the piano and placed it in front of him. It read Bach *Minuet in G*. She played it first. "Now, what is the first note on the page?"

"Um, F, no, um," Damien stumbled over his decision, "um, G." Damien unconfidently bleated, but knew it was not right, because the note on the staff was clearly an F, but the name at the top of the page said G. He hated being put on the spot, with the twinging sensation that accompanied it. He had been playing by ear from the beginning. Now he was being tested to read the sheet music in front of him. It was reading the sound, a concept that was turning it all inside out.

"Where is it on the staff?" Mrs White probed. Damien felt his heart flip, she wouldn't re-question if he had been right.

"It is an F." He shot out in a bid to re-correct his misstep.

"Don't doubt yourself Damien. You were right the first time. And what is after the treble clef?"

"A sharp symbol."

"So what note does the piece start with?" Mrs White coaxed.

"F sharp."

"Now see this hole in the head of our starting note, followed by a dot?" Damien nodded in full attention. "This is called a dotted half note which is a half note tied to a quarter note and totals three counts. This is why you see a three four. That means three counts in four per bar."

Mrs White placed her fingers on the piano and as she played slowly counted out the timing of each finger placement within each measure of the piece, "one...two three, one...two three," protruding her *ones* out into eternal rectitude. He recognised the piece. He had played it before, but not like this, with his eyes up rather than down.

"Now you try," Mrs White persuaded. "Posture, Damien." She hinted gently tapping her fingertips to the small of his back. He immediately sat upright. "Gently, now. Just with your right hand first. And try to follow your eyes on the notes."

Damien played. He stumbled on the fifth note. He twisted his mouth.

"That's ok, and again." Mrs White encouraged.

Damien started again and let his fingers roll across the keys.

Mrs White placed both hands on the piano and played with them together. "Now, with the left hand," she began to play in demonstration, before turning to Damien, "off you go."

Damien copied her example.

"And both hands together. Keep your eyes up."

Damien played its replica. It wasn't perfect, he stumbled, he stopped, he started again. He played it for the sixth time until he got it right.

"Good boy." Mrs White turned and gave him a smile.

He collected his music book and new pieces for practice. As soon as he returned home, he raced into his room and pulled his keyboard out. He plunged his fingers everywhere and anywhere until he made up his own little melody, a playful ring into the quiet room that somehow made the walls escape their greyish off white, pervading the toneless space into his own minute incubator. The sound rebuffed like a pillow making a cosy hidey hole of a cave he could saturate with a resonance of his own creation.

It was at times in competition or sometimes in collaboration with music coming from the living room whenever Frank or Claudia put on the record player. The house was charged with music when a happy mood paired itself with the day they may have had. Claudia matched chorales with Frank's Moonlight Serenade[3]. It would drift into his room and his subconscious allowed it to seep. It was a sign of inhabitation, and danced like the steps of beings who were only the short distance of another room.

When the long stretches of silence pervaded, he knew how to bring back the footsteps. When the darkness descended and the music stopped, he would imagine them back to life, bouncing around the room like fireflies dancing in the ink of night.

---

[3] Miller, Glenn. Moonlight Serenade. Bluebird. 1939.

CHAPTER SIX

When the sun had closed its eyes and he couldn't play outside, his room became his fortification. There he preoccupied himself with every kept trinket. He scavenged from the base of his box of tricks and sculpted a world away from his own, all in the space in front of him. He had constructed a small battalion, with two sides pitched against the other, sprawled in front of him, sitting on his bedroom floor. He struck one soldier down and slayed another, scouring them over the grains in the wood floor and blasting them into false oblivion. The hell was palpable. It was real to him. The harder he bashed them about the better he felt. Authentic. The lights in the room suddenly went out.

Utter blackness thwarted the scene with a fright. No light was coming from anywhere else in the house. It was quickly followed by a small gasp and murmurings from his grandparents in the living room, their feet scuffling across the floorboards like heavy footed mice.

"It's just a blackout." Claudia called from the living room.

A brownish orange light started to seep its way through Damien's door, as his eyes tried to frantically search for something tangible in the room, frightened.

"Are you alright?" Claudia emerged holding a candle, its subtle ray moistened the air with its chestnut syrup.

"Yes," Damien muttered his heart palpitations subsiding. "What happened?"

"Oh, a transformer has probably blown."

"What's a transformer?"

"It's where the power comes from."

A hissing spraying sound punched through the house and a white light crept in. Frank appeared in Damien's doorway holding a lamp, its bright gas-white light piercing their eyes. "You want to come in with us into the living room? It will be pretty dark in here otherwise."

"Um," he hesitated. Then Claudia interjected.

"Here, you can stay in here with this candle." She placed the candle on the floor just in front of him cascading its colour of pawpaw across his face. "But be careful. I'll come back and check on you before bed."

Damien was glad of the respite they gave. He didn't want to leave his haven.

Claudia and Frank walked back to the living room leaving Damien in peace. He was suddenly caught up in an enraptured feeling of daring, with the scary notion of being alone in a blackened room, its darkness pierced only by a flickering candle light. He had never been in this position before. Never been in a blackout.

His battalion gleaned a whole new lustre. No longer was it a visible array of copper toy soldiers on a boy's bedroom floor. Everything around the figurines was blacked out, even the floor upon which they stood. Muddied. They were visible only by the reflected light that glimmered on their shiny metallic chests. A glisten on their faces he imagined reflected the strain and sweat of the battle they endured.

"Swoosh! Swish! Pow! Pow!" Damien hurtled out as he

grappled one soldier against another. He smashed, he bashed until he scattered them into disarray. The candle flame burst its light like simmering explosions within the field of traipsing soldiers and lit them up as they were razed. The flame's conjectures caught his eye. The way it flickered, moved around in small swirls, trying to escape its wick, being perpetually held, drawn back to its point of origin. He looked down at one of the defeated soldiers, lying prostrate near the base of the candle, how the light sashayed across his flagellated form, nicking his armour's edges. Damien's eyes diverted up to the candle, then back down to the toy, seeing if he could catch the flame's belly dance being mimicked in the light on his chest. He picked up the soldier and held him just above the candle, watching the way the light revealed the intricacies of his makeup. But the closer he held it, his metal turned more orange, his face looked in dread. A face of battle-ready strength turned to a face ravaged with terror. He lowered the soldier further and imagined him burning, then he pulled him away, dropping him to the floor. He touched his fingers over his armoured chest, feeling the hotness the flame had left.

Damien lay sideways on the floor with his head on his hands and in a trance stared at the candle, watching its dance. He lifted his hand up over the top letting it gently hover, allowing it to suck in its warmth, then lowered his hand further and could feel it getting hot and knew to withdraw before allowing it to sting. There was a happy medium, the medium of where warmness lay. Not too high, not too low. He stared at the point above the flame's tip where he had held his hand. Out of the blackness behind it, there appeared to be another, gracefully hovering hers on the other side of him.

He blinked and when he opened his eyes it was gone. He squinted his eyes in their haze, sure of what he saw through the black speckle dust of the space behind the light. There was nothing there. He sat upright, sure there had been. He squinted and stared harder. Again, nothing was there. Wiping his eyes, he shook his head trying to rid the creeping furrow in his brow. He knew something had been there. He felt it.

He lay his body back down on the floor and rested the side of his head on his hand and stared at the flame. He knew what had been there. He knew what he saw. He would wait for it to come back again.

The scent of oiled wood overworn by the scuffed smell of old shoes tinged with pine gently laced his nostrils the longer he lay with his head close to the floor. It was in conflict with the Valerian of sleep and the heavy vapour of wax. He fought it. There was no chance now that he would close his eyes. No chance to miss what he knew he saw.

He watched the wax pool then drip from the black of the wick. It formed a hemline at the base of the saucer like the train of a bridal gown. He reached his hand out and pressed his finger leaving his print in the soft warm wax to place a tag upon the candle for a place he wanted to return. He couldn't fight the weight of his eyes any more. They closed of their own accord.

CHAPTER SEVEN

A marble delicately rolled across the hardwood. Then another. Their bearing was at the front door. Damien lolled on the floor staring at the direction of the door as he let marbles flick from his fingers. He let them roll out from under his hands, as he stared like a liquid tonic elixir had drugged him into a bleary-eyed stupor, their motion hypnotizing him. One after the other, letting them roll, waiting for them to hit the door, hearing the ping and knock as they bounced off the wood. What he was doing he didn't know. Passing the time, what else does a bored little boy do, wading through six years. Waiting in earnest for the door to maybe open, waiting for the marbles to miraculously be knocked back in his direction. Some form of acknowledgement that there was indeed something on the other side. Something worth waiting for, something to come get him. Get him and take him out of there.

Then like a bolt out of no-where, at some point between marble gazing and sleeping, there she was. Cynthia.

She had turned up one afternoon after he had arrived home from school and was shocked to see her sitting on the sofa in the living room, drinking tea with Claudia. Too startled to feel elated by the sighting, instead he looked at her dubiously. Tricks of his eyesight had deluded him before. Was this a blind spot, merely an apparition? But there was Rory toddling on the floor in front of them, with his soft brown hair and pudgy arms swinging about within an arms-length of her, his mother.

"Oh there you are," his grandmother exclaimed with a stern calm. "Come and see who is here." She gave him a 'be a good boy' look as her eyes directed him to the person sitting at the opposite end of the room.

Cynthia sat on the sofa with a smile being forced through a heartbreak her eyes couldn't hide as they squinted back their wateriness staring in his direction. "Hello sweetheart," she dispersed with a muted hesitation. "Come over here, let me see you." She extended her arm unfurling her hand like the silver sided leaf of an olive.

Damien watched the gesture of his mother's hands, avoiding her eyes as they searched his face. He wanted to run forward and collapse himself into her crying. Instead he walked up to her dutifully with his head down and felt those same hands wrap around the back of his shoulders and pull him into her, as she gave him a kiss on his cheek, pressing him ever so softly into her chest. To feel her face against his was like the softest velvet encasing the most exquisite gift. As he withdrew back from her he thought he could hear her slightness of breath, wasn't sure if she was weeping. The momentary tenderness was somehow impinged by a fraught-ness, an anxiety. An anxiety that pervaded the space between the two of them as soon as he stood back from her.

"Your mother has some exciting news." Claudia extended encouragingly.

"That's right. Fully fledged secretary now." She smiled at him with a shy diverting gaze before turning to her mother, "at least I can now rent a better place." She coyly stroked at Rory's overalls, as though cleaning a crumb that wasn't there.

"That's good isn't it Damien. You can stop over and visit now." Claudia tilted her head at him in reassurance, one that infused him with a hope like no other – he would finally be out of here and back home with his mother. But what did she mean by the word *visit*.

"So tell me what you have been up to?" Cynthia tried, in a minimalist fervour. "Grandma tells me you are really good at the piano."

"Yes." Damien nodded shyly, trying to suppress the knot in his throat as Claudia diplomatically ejected herself from the scene.

"You will have to play me something." She uttered with tender breath.

"Yes." Damien acknowledged, but his thoughts quickly jettisoned back to the *visit* comment half wondering what it meant and if it meant what it meant – a union - if it *was* possible, or an empty remark. He hoped not an empty remark with the wrong choice of word.

"And you have been doing very well at school. I spoke to Mrs Fletcher."

Damien's face perked up.

"She said you are at the top of the class."

"Yes." Damien nodded in a quietly concerted but proud fashion, allowing a smile to break through.

"That's my smart boy. I knew you would be." She said with understated simplicity.

Claudia walked back into the room and produced a plate of cookies she had baked.

"Here you go Damien," she offered before placing them on the coffee table in front of them. Damien grabbed a cookie and stood there picking at it between his teeth, loitering there in front of them both, not sure what he was supposed to do, what was meant to happen next. The silence then dictated it.

"Go on, show your mother how you can play," Claudia eyed Damien toward the piano, then turned to Cynthia, "he knows Bach and some Mozart."

Damien relented and placed the cookie back on the plate.

"Come here, wipe your hands first," Claudia handed him a tea towel and he scuffed the top of his fingers before walking over to the piano, seated himself on the stool, then lifted up the lid, placing his fingers gently on the keys.

His grandmother looked on encouragingly and Cynthia in anticipation as he started to play a simple piece by Bach. The notes dinged into the awkward air, like the chiming bell rung before taking the holy sacrament, instead being played at a wake, displaced.

"See, I told you he was good." Claudia conceded. "Mrs White has been very complimentary."

"Oh well done. Play it again." Cynthia enthused and Damien yielded. The second attempt breathed life into it.

Cynthia clapped her hands together as Damien turned around and walked back to collect the cookie from the plate. "That's my boy. You *are* very good." Rory toppled onto his side and Cynthia gave a gushing whoop before quickly collecting him up off the floor and swinging him onto her lap, holding him tightly kissing him on the cheek. "Come and say hello to your little brother." Cynthia smiled.

Damien too looked at Rory dubiously, as the toddler tried to grab at the cookie half eaten out of his mother's hand in want. Damien walked up cautiously. Cynthia could see his hesitation.

"It's ok," she eyed him reflecting his nervousness, "would you like to come and say hello?"

Damien peered at him curiously, "nah," and sat on the

arm chair to the side, biting tentatively at the cookie.

"Now," Cynthia pushed on, "I'll take you out on the weekend. Would you like that?"

Damien looked up at her not sure what she had just asked. He hadn't seen her for so many months, wasn't sure if she was coming back and all of a sudden she was offering a second coming, he repeated her question back to her, sure she was in fact misinforming herself of her own situation.

"You want to take *me* out on the weekend?"

"Yes, would you like that?"

"*This* weekend?" He said bewildered.

"Yes," Cynthia looked at him a little perplexed.

"OK," Damien responded looking up at her blankly. He didn't know what else to say. His mother's exact whereabouts had been enshrouded in such mystery that he wasn't sure whether this new mystery – her wanting to take him out – was one which would materialise into resolved fact. It made him somersault back over the word *visit* sure *that* was the misunderstanding. All meaning divorced the reality of the words. The former didn't reconcile with the latter. What was she here for? To take him or to just take him out? He tried with his might to shatter his own questions.

When she drove off in her car, there was a painful energy fighting him to suppress the confusion inside, but it wasn't enough to kill his excitement. *Here she is. She is going to take me out on the weekend. She is going to take me home.*

That night he started to put all the toys from his windowsill, the corner of his room and under his bed in a box, so he would have everything in order and ready for easy carting to take to the car with him.

CHAPTER EIGHT

Damien slapped Patrick hard on the back making him wince and as he was shutting his eyes, he snatched the eraser off Patrick's desk.

"Why did you do that for?" Patrick half coughed out, as Damien held a cheeky grin and started to laugh in amusement. "What?" Patrick smiled back at him, not realising the missing piece from his desk.

Damien couldn't contain himself and continued to splutter in laughter bursts. Patrick looked about him, felt behind his back in case he had stuck something on it, looked around the desk, and then noticed his eraser was missing from on top of it.

"Hey, you took my eraser. Give it back." Patrick playfully insisted to his desk mate, while Damien continued to reign supreme in his chortles.

"Give it back," he started to fidget at Damien's hidden hands. Mrs Fletcher entered the room and the two of them sat to attention, their faces red with compulsion, before the eraser suddenly flew through the air in front of Patrick's eyes making him momentarily lose his militaristic gaze. They both emitted a restrained half laugh that caused Mrs Fletcher to look about the room. But two seasoned experts in flying under the radar were never going to be caught in any kind of mischief.

Damien's mood had lifted somewhat since the visitation. Since the glimmer of hope was able to deliver. He found himself energised, more alert to the spring in his step and ability to tear down the schoolyard out-chasing Patrick and laughing. Laughing at the games the two of them played. Laughing so hard, he wasn't sure from where it came. Too young to understand the smile caught on his face, how it got there with each passing day until the weekend when she promised she was coming to take him back. It captured the attention of Mrs Fletcher, but in some bizarre form of a backhanded compliment, it only encouraged her to pick on him more.

"Well, aren't we in a fine mood today Mr Zane," she boomed through the room. "Now come to the front of the class and read the first page," she beseeched, holding a book up into the air.

Damien trudged up to the front, not wanting this new form of indictment. He took the book from her and opened the cover. He looked over the first line. He understood the words and started to read out the first sentence, nervously stumbling over words he knew well. Knew so well, they were too simple for him, its rhyme and meter too slow for his pace. But it was the eyes staring at him that made him want to retreat. Eager eyes gazing upon him. Was it in awe? Beguiling respect? Intense ridicule? He had tried so hard to stay out of everyone's way as a measure of avoidance of little whispers, he suddenly felt a discomfort when placed in full view of everyone. He felt his face flush and was glad when it was over and he could hide back behind his desk in the middle of the classroom.

As the class ended and the children stood up and moved away from their desks, Mrs Fletcher called out, yet again, as he was heading toward the door. "Damien," she called in a softer tone. She pulled out a batch of about five books from her desk. "I want you to have these." The books were plentiful. He wasn't certain why she was giving them to him, what she wanted him to do with them. "I know you can get through these," she cajoled.

He nodded respectfully to her before turning around. He was happy to accept a challenge she set. If it was a nod to outpace everyone else in the room, he would duly dive in.

"OK," he noted and cumbersomely walked out.

He stopped and knelt on the floor of the hallway and shoved them into his bag, before swinging it onto his back and running as fast as possible out the doors, like a delirious kid-goat knocked out into a field scrambling to keep up with the other animals that were nothing like him.

He headed straight home and committed at least an hour to piano practise, an hour for homework and was allowed half an hour of television before dinner in which he was glued. In between times he ventured outside where no-one else was, to avoid the quietness of his room. Within his room he could create his own world. Outside he could make whole adventures.

He deliberately played within eyeshot to demonstrate he was ok in the face of how he felt. A game of pretend happiness. To make sure they could still see him. That they didn't forget he was there. If he knew their eyes were on him it was equivalent of his eyes being on them – to see that *they* were still there and hadn't left him too. Even if it was the sound of them, then that was enough to rid him of his fear that they were gone. To play make believe in front of them was the only thing he could do, after the weekend had come and gone and Cynthia had indeed taken him out for the day, only to return him back.

She took him for a milkshake with Rory, then for a play in the park. He remembered the last time she had taken him there. She had pushed him on the swing. Now his legs were his master. As the afternoon closed, rather than a walk around to her house, she walked him back to her car. The sight and the sound of her press and pull at the steel handle to open the back door made the milk at the back of his throat feel like puke. One that choked him. He felt tight in his chest as he sat in the back trying to recollect in his head all the sentences she had spoken when she sat opposite him as he sucked on his straw. Was there something he missed? Or was there something she could not see in front of her?

The grey blue light of Sunday stroked his walls. He stared at the box of possessions he had packed in the moonlight with a furrow in his brow as he lay back in his bed. The furrow grew deeper with the down turn of his mouth, the accrual of running thoughts pounding. Maybe next week, he thought. He would leave the box as it was. Maybe next week he would make the move.

*

A scurrying six-year-old was never part of the home Claudia thought she would inhabit in this part of her life. She looked on at him as he played in the front yard while she busied herself potting geraniums on the front porch. Her heart was equal parts joy, for the little grandson now within her care who extended sunshine into her life, and heartbreak for her daughter, full of fear for her future. Claudia's life with Frank was a simple one. Damien hadn't complicated it. He was quiet, well behaved, no trouble. His father had complicated it. Or was it Cynthia. She didn't want to take sides. Didn't want to point the finger. She reserved her judgement for the Lord and no-one else.

She made a pact with herself not to discuss with Damien

what it was about his mother, why she didn't take him with her. She had explained it once as a necessary action so she could keep on going and that was as much as he needed to know. He seemed happy enough, so there was no need to push in a narrative for which he was better off not knowing more. Her thoughts, her prayers were reserved for hoping things would turn out right. That the Lord would forgive. This was life and this was the way it was to be accepted. And Frank followed suit. He liked having Damien around. Frank was saddened when his daughter and the man she married were to be no more a pair. He remembered the day she had turned up on the doorstep in tears. He didn't like the blight it cast. But the cards were disproportionately in place and tumbled like dominos, with the last domino kicked out of the pack being Damien. Being the oldest, he had every confidence his grandson would be every bit the young boy ahead of his years who could exist in unfortunate circumstances and be a beacon of admiration for his younger sibling, despite its compromise. *In time*. Frank told himself. In time he hoped he'd understand why. *It won't be forever.* They were always in his prayers.

They never missed a Sunday of paying respect to the Lord and to their small community. Frank played the tuba in the church band and was keen to get Damien involved. Claudia wanted him to start participating in the choir. She had made Damien have a go at singing at one of his Sunday school classes and was encouraged to hear he had quite a sweetly angelic voice.

He would be the prize and reinstate the gilt bow pinned to her chest when wearing her Sunday best, seeing her grandson do them proud in front of a town too caught up in whispers for the past year. And Damien naturally conceded to his new-found duty.

"Is that Cynthia's little boy up there Claudia?" A

whispered voice chirped to the side of Claudia's ear, as the small group of children were gathered at the altar for Easter celebrations.

Claudia smiled and nodded politely, "yes, it certainly is." She couldn't help her pride radiate peach upon her cheeks. They all stood as a congregation and together sang The Lord Is My Shepherd before retreating to their seats. Their angel's breath at the base of the steeple was annulled by the creak of the wooden pews. The collection of children in their white smocks like puffed out marshmallows with liquorice collars were the candied gilding in a celebration of life after death.

"God shall grant eternal redemption for he who commands a life in His footsteps, repents all his sins and impurities and denies all temptation. The Lord our grace died for all of us, so our children may walk in the light of His being the day He offered us His eternal protection. May He deliver us from evil. Amen."

Damien watched the pastor as he stood behind him at the altar with a crowd of dulcet faces before him. The words shot through the back of his head, muffled through indirection. He didn't know what any of it meant. Someone died for everyone. The Lord. He wasn't sure who that really was. But He was important – according to everyone. They *had* dressed for the occasion. They *always* dressed for the occasion that was Sunday. He tried to unpick the meaning of the pastor's words as low mumbles tumbled out the mouths of the flock in repetition. "Children may walk in the light". That sounded like the yellow brick road. He thought of Dorothy and Toto. "Protection" was the wand from the Good Fairy of the North. "Deliver us from" – the phrase. That didn't make sense. "Deliver us to" made more sense, like "I delivered a letter to you", a sentence he learnt at school. "Evil" he pondered. The tornado.

They went to a local coffee shop after church for coffee

and cake. It was the only thing worth the hour long wait – the cake. A place of Little Bo Peep curtains pulled back against the window panes and mustard vinyl seats. Damien was surprised to see Cynthia and Rory sitting in a booth waiting for them. The first weekend she took him out left him mystified. Each time subsequent more so because they seemed irregular in their intention, leaving him uncertain. There was indefiniteness. Hesitation. His weekends with her seemed forced, a rehearsed gesture for which he was always waiting for something more. The real thing. Then she drove him back home again or waited until Frank or Claudia came to pick him up. And today she didn't come to church – a place she had always been. She seemed scared of something. She wondered if it was him.

"Do you like singing in the choir?" Cynthia asked in a nervously applauding fashion as he sank his teeth into a large piece of chocolate cake.

"Mm hmm," he nodded scoffing down the piece in his mouth.

"I'm going to show him the tuba over summer and then he'll be able to join in the band, won't you kiddo," Frank enthusiastically contributed.

Damien smiled as he mumbled through a mouth of cake, "the tuba is too big," though it was the perfect sized instrument to get him noticed. He would never be invisible.

"You can handle it," Frank said in jest before relenting, "well maybe in a few years then."

"Yes, we've got more piano practice in the meantime, first things first." Claudia consoled.

As he sat chomping on his piece of cake, he watched Rory nuzzle beside Cynthia, who was occasionally slipping miniscule pieces of meringue into his tiny mouth. The adults started to trail off into their own language, Damien becoming oblivious to their menagerie of contained adult conversation to which he did not belong. He sometimes caught the odd furtive look in his direction by Cynthia. The quickness of her eyes in diversion made him sure she held her interest in Rory rather than him. He got up from the table and excused himself.

"Can I go outside?" He asked Claudia.

"Yes, off you go."

Damien raced outside into the street. The sun was sharp. Out on the pavement, he paced up and down and walked to the side of the coffee shop. In the small laneway he found a discarded bottle cap, glistening its copper flanks in the sunlight and picked it up. One lob up, one hurl down, up, down, fling up higher. Lob. Toss. Chuck. Sunspots glazed his retina the moments after he followed its ascent. He watched it slam against the concrete path louder and louder each time he tossed it higher and higher absorbing its clanking ping. He picked it up and threw it hard, slamming it against the brick wall at the back of the shop. It bounced back and shunted with a screeching metallic peal. He leaned down to pluck it up off the ground. The screw top was scratched and dinted as he examined what he had done to it. He traced his finger over its ridges and scratches. He threw it hard to the concrete again hearing its metal ring and stomped on the top of it trying to crush it further into the ground beneath his feet. A rigour in his chest and an aggression deep in his heart burrowed it further in. But it was a hard piece of metal and as he skimmed his foot away, it was the concrete underfoot that broke. Broken like the crushed foundations of a house. He was like the bottle cap within it, scratched, rolling around within its tomb alert to the loose base upon which it stood. It made being outside a freedom where the ground was tactile and unmoving. But inside was where the other bottle caps assembled. He wandered back into the coffee shop out of prescribed order.

He hoped they were finished with their conversation. He was bored. He intensely disliked church and this was just one long drawn out affair of a Sunday. He sat back down in the chair and picked at the remaining crumbs of cake on his plate, with flushed cheeks.

"Would you like chocolate cake for your birthday?" Cynthia suddenly proliferated in front of him as she watched him lick pieces of crumb from his fingers.

Damien looked up at her with a start unprepared for the question. "Um," he stumbled, "yes, I think so." He pondered. He nodded his head. He hadn't even been thinking of his birthday. It was only at her having prompted it that made him realise - yes - it was his birthday soon. How could he ever forget it? He couldn't.

"Lucky number seven," Cynthia said smiling at him.

He was suddenly thrust with a profound magical thought – was there something underlying why his mother had asked him about his birthday cake? Was it a hint? A surprise hidden within the code of her smile. He felt a brief moment of excitement. Maybe there was a surprise in store for the thing he'd been waiting for. He tried to read it in her face.

There was something in Cynthia's hazel green eyes that made him drink in their sparkle. Her eyes hadn't sparkled at him in a while. Their downcast forlornness before she had left hit him with a shudder so sharp he had to look away. It was in contrast to the woman sitting in front of him now. He was consumed by her eyes when she looked upon him, curious as to whether she saw him, *really* saw him, drank him in as much as he did her, then acutely aware of when she looked away from him, averting her eyes as though she was in the company of someone she was ashamed to be with, shy of him. She had the prettiest smile that was like a crocus flower before nightfall – he missed it desperately once it was gone. It was what was hidden inside its cover of darkness that lay the most invaluable thing of all. A new pain of awareness was that he couldn't afford it because no-one was willing to offer him a price.

When he got home he knelt by his bed and closed his eyes. Prayers pathed a way to something, so he was told. More like a path from. It was like walking inside from the cold night air. A walk away from a price.

CHAPTER NINE

He pulled out the mini torch from under his pillow. It was the present John had given him earlier in the day for his seventh birthday. He had recounted the tale of the blackout to John in great detail. Detail leaving John hard to forget. It was a gift in lieu of the effort of recital rather than for its impending aid. Damien hid it as soon as he got it and now that night had brought the darkest shadow he pulled it out and switched it on. He began to flash it around the ceiling, as he looked up into the cavernous dark, lying flat on his back on the bed. He made slow spinning circles, then swiftly flashed the light in zig zag patterns weaving across the space above him. It made a sparkle each time it traversed the glass of the overhead lightbulb, switched off in its invisibility. He repeated the same patterns, making a swishing sound from his mouth with every movement, winding from a hum of circles to a more laser like slash with each linear stroke. The dazzle of light was hypnotizing and placed him into a trance. He flicked the torch switch on and off and stopped and stared in the vacuum of black.

"Oh there you are", he said peering down to the side.

Ava was sitting cross legged on the floor, staring up at the ceiling, waiting for the recommencement of the light show. She hadn't been at his birthday party during the day. He didn't know where she had been. The only people there were his family, Patrick and a handful of his class mates. They spent the day running around the backyard chomping on chocolate and candies sucking on the blood of sugar cane.

"It looks better from here" he said, as he scooted over in his bed, making room for her to lie beside him. She pulled herself up off the floor and lay on top of the bed, shuffling close to his left-hand side, looking up in unison with him.

He switched the torch back on and started to flash the light again moving it around with its beam like a lonely lighthouse on a cape.

"See. Look there." He pointed definitively to the centre of the ceiling. "It flashes more when I go like this." He swiped the light across the centre crisscrossing the light bulb and once again it sparkled. It was bright in the darkness, scattering potbellied shadow puppets in the crevices at the back.

"Oh yeah," Ava noted with a spark of excitement as sharp as the light. "Do it again."

He swirled and twirled the light and they lay there mesmerised until he switched it off, both of them quietly staring into the dark.

"Well I can show you something," Ava piped up in the quietness of the room. "But you have to stay still. Close your eyes."

Damien did what he was told and was ready and waiting. Ava leaned in closer to him, and he could feel the lengths of her hair tickle his neck. A smile sprung on his face and he forced himself not to giggle. She leaned in closer moving her face close to his and brushed her eyelashes in a rapid flutter against the ball of his cheek. He couldn't retain himself and spluttered a bluster of giggles which Ava duly accompanied as she collapsed back beside him on the bed.

"It's a butterfly kiss," she said with a grin.

"Yeah I know," he said hiding his.

He held up his hand close to his face and fluttered his lashes furiously against the palm of his hand, feeling the tickling sensation.

He picked up the torch and switched it on shining it into the palm of his hand, wondering if butterfly kisses left a mark. Instead he followed the trail of lines with the torch, its map of roads, rivers and networks, striking out like streaks of lava from a lychee skin until it transformed into a river of blue then flipped his hand over and shone the light through it. The edges glowed a red-orange plasma around the outline of his hand. He switched it off and the room went black.

"It's better in the dark," Damien announced to the room.

"Except you can't see anything nincompoop," Ava chortled.

"Yes you can. You can see better. Look!" Damien emphasised as though pointing something out in the blackened space.

"Where?"

"There!" He tested.

"Where there?" she bemused.

"Here!" He bounced on the light again flashing into his face like a ghoul, growling, then started to laugh. His smile disappeared from his face as he flashed the light on and off, before letting the room fall into the hue of silence.

In perfect stillness there was nothing to torment the darkness. This night he felt unafraid of it. He couldn't see in the black and in the quiet he couldn't hear. He liked the quiet tonight. He could feel his presence within it.

He let out a sigh, rolled over and pulled the covers up

across his shoulders and tried to find a succulent spot on his pillow for his head to sink. He allowed the hypoglycaemic side effects of the day's sugar binge to plunge him into sluggish sleep. The flashes and sparkles inside his head streaked themselves into treacle-like fibres like the wool of a white cotton candy. His shoulder snuggled in between the bed and the pillow. The torch rolled off the covers and rested in the empty place beside him.

CHAPTER TEN

The time he spent in his father's car that last summer was the cosiest place he could have inhabited. John had picked Damien up every so often during the holidays and taken him for a drive which reactivated the remnants of memory. Sometimes for an hour or two driving along the highway reignited a whole new imagined lifetime. It was in these moments he felt he was with someone he wanted to be with.

The mud crust from the wipers on the windscreen streaked the road ahead. It clung wherever they went. It marked the view by marking the car of the two people it carried. Every angle was an artscape in silt.

There was an 8-track player fitted in the dash and John slotted in tapes of his favourite artists. He played The Grateful Dead and The Doors. They were the ones Damien remembered, because his father liked them too. John waxed lyrical about what the songs were about, when they came out and how important it was to listen, really listen to the sound, the tone, the melody. The tempo John created within their travelling cavalcade was what was palpable – a pulse that beat out *you and me*.

The player periodically jammed eating the tape leading it to be pulled out in a Medusa's tangle.

"Damn that tape." John twilled the cartridge in front of him. "Gotta be something better than this Damien. When the tape gets dirty it breaks."

Damien listened on in reverence.

"They have been selling these new decks in the store for cassettes. That's the big thing for stereo. I got to get me a car with one."

John told Damien what songs he should learn how to play on the piano. It made Damien excited at the thought of what he could do, was endlessly enthralled by the excitement he read in John's face and the sound of his voice as he described the rapture of the musicians he played out to him on the player.

"Hear that?" John pointed to the deck with its freight-train drum.

Damien looked up, curiously awake to it.

"It's the build-up," before he let his hand mellow itself like stroking the mane of a foal, "and then phfeuwww…" he softly pumped out the air from his lips like a warm low wave.

It was an enthusiasm easy to become ensconced in. Damien was taken.

All men have dreams. Maybe he had wanted to be one of those artists he so enamoured. John played the guitar, but it was more of a quiet hobby reserved for the spare moments in his days outside of work. Damien's gift for music might turn into a new dream.

John pointed at the track in the dash as a high-strung riff bleated out.

Damien smiled back.

They stopped in to the music store in town to replace the cartridge bent out of shape. The jangle of a rock track played from behind the counter as the sheen of the ceiling lights reflected off the waxed vinyl covers, with their tangerine and lemon loop titles on chocolate. It dazzled an understated charm of hominess. The store smelt of cardboard and plastic and tobacco ash. And its carpet contained the sound, absorbing and swallowing each beat and crescendo. It was an encyclopedia underfoot. A book of songs like the ones John played on the deck. He didn't want to leave. As he dawdled among the shelves waiting he cast his eye over a cover of The Byrds[4]. Men hanging back on steps in front of a desert with a mammoth rock. Cowboys. He wondered was that where they went when they hit the road – a desert that looked like the bed of an ocean – to places like nowhere he had ever seen.

"Have you ever been to the beach?" Damien asked when they were back in the car.

"Never been that far." John relented.

"Is there a beach near here?" The closest Damien had gotten to water was the local swimming pool, the river and the creek.

"Not in this State." He gave an understated laugh. It sounded like remorse.

"How do you get there?"

"You take this road we're on and you just keep going." He looked down at Damien. Damien wondered how long it would take.

The car bumped along roads with a pale sky and plump clouds. With the windows down the scent of the turf from fresh harvested crops breezed through. The tar from the road in the hot summer heat evaporated in and gripped his skin. When it rained, the rolled up windows contained the Armor-

---

[4] Album cover The Byrds: *Untitled*. Columbia. 1970

All® dash scent and his seat couldn't hide its leather hugged by velveteen. It was the equivalent of being curled up in an armchair.

The gas station stops he coveted. Damien helped fill the gas tank. They were the best days. He didn't have to wait in the car like a kid. He got out, walked around to the side, popped the cap and pulled the nozzle from the bowser and slunk it in as John watched on. It was the work of a man. The son of a man. He was a man like him. He followed John in to pay and if there was a new comic book on the stand at the counter, John bought it for him.

But there were only so many stops. Until it stopped. Just like the needle in the dash that slowly collapsed its arm as the fuel tank read low, the road also slowed on its final bend.

The summer came and went with the collective ferocity of a tornado with all the foundations and sweet spots ripped out and hurled away with it when he was delivered back to Claudia and Frank's front door. He wanted to run back to the car, as though he was mistaking it for his father's, before it left the driveway that last week. But here was where he was delivered and here he was supposedly meant to remain. The sound of the car's tyres driving across the gravel out of the driveway crunched away the melodies and hums that had so softly inhabited his ears and his brain. All he could hope for was that the time happened again.

He sat back in his room and mulled over all the questions he should have come up with, could have asked that would have made him need another day or two more, another reason to stay an hour longer so he could say everything he needed to say the right way and in turn give him all the answers he wanted, all the time he needed. Even if he had to ask questions for which he already knew their answers. He stared at the jar on his sill. The marble jar for tadpoles now housed six pebbles he had collected from the brook. Collected for recollection, some sort anyway. Would they give him an answer? He looked past the jar to the sky through the window. There was no writing in the sky or writing on rock that was telling him what he should have done better to make it last.

The days leading up to school return were empty and felt as long as the whole of the summer itself. The vacant black eerie feeling from months before started to creep right back. *It*. He walked from his room outside and up the side of the house and back again. Then again and again. Pacing. Until its inactivity overtook him.

He sat on the step at the back of the house where for hours he traced a path with his eyes on the sediment below and followed the trail of a solitary ant, watching it carry a heavy load. A crumb, like the clusters of grains of sand, too big for its body, but somehow it managed to make its journey, then untethered itself from the weight when it found its way home. His back ached sitting in such a constrained position for so long. He stood up and walked back inside – the only place he could go.

He fingered through the left overs of a jam cake Claudia had made. Its jam was cold from the fridge. He licked the stickiness from his fingers and withdrew from picking at it any further lest she caught him. He hoped she would make another next week and surprise him with a slice in his lunchbox. There had to be a sweetener somewhere, when he returned to the way things were mapped out to be.

CHAPTER ELEVEN

A shrill sound pierced from a distance followed by a soft thud that woke Damien with a start. He rose from his pillow and peered his head toward the window from where he thought it had come. Peeling back the bed sheet he scuffed his head with his hands and slowly stepped onto the hardwood floor and delicately tiptoed to the window. He looked around outside and couldn't see anything remiss, until he peered downward toward the ground. There outside the window he could see something black as a clump, soft and feather-like.

He gathered his shoes slipping them on his feet without socks and grabbed a pullover from the wardrobe stretching his arms through its woollen sleeves and clumped haphazardly to the door.

Soggy leaves made a barely audible sluicing sound upon the dewed grass as Damien slowly walked around to the side of the house to the window of his bedroom. There below it he saw what looked like a dead black bird, hunched and lifeless on the edge of the flowerbed, its black feathers shiny like coal gently flickering in an almost absent breeze. He was sure it was dead. It must have been. He leaned in closer crouching down and curved his head around to see if it was breathing, moving. He picked up a small twig nesting in the flowers wet with the morning dew and cautiously protruded it toward the bird, hesitant. He jumped back slightly as he gave it a quick prod. But it did not react, laying without a stir. He prodded it again. Nothing.

Frank was around the back, loading sacks into the truck. Damien trundled over having heard him from the side.

"Grandpa," he quietly motioned, "I think I found something."

"What's that Damien?" Frank slid a heap of canvas sacking into a corner.

"Beneath my window," he pointed down to the side, "a bird."

"Show me."

Damien illustrated the way and walked down to the side with his grandfather. The sky was grey overhead with slowly parting cracks.

"See," Damien pointed to the black lump.

"Ah, right," Frank knelt down. "Had better clear him away then."

"What happened to him?"

"Probably another bird got him." Frank walked back toward the truck and brought around a shovel, scooping the bird up in it. "Looks like a raven."

Damien peeked at it inquisitively as its neck flopped back on the metal. Its two small slits for eyes were closed, it looked peaceful, asleep, but its beak with its sharp stout curve made it a stark abstraction to the soft down of its feathers so shiny and black. That's when he noticed a bloody gash on the shoulder of its wing tacking a clump of feathers like a sticky glue. He looked up at his window and could see a tiny streak of red upon it.

"An eagle probably got him." Frank calmly asserted as he

walked the bird to the outer garden. "I'll bury him over there."

Damien followed as Frank plopped the bird back on the ground and started to dig a hole by a Crepe Myrtle, breaching the soil with his shovel. Scooping the bird back up again, he placed it in the hole, its neck flopped back as it found its resting place in the scooped-out earth. Damien watched the closed eye of the bird before the dirt rained back down on top burying it in a shallow tomb.

What if he is not dead? He looks asleep to me. Maybe he is just sleeping. Damien thought in his head. But he didn't want to mention such a notion to his grandfather when it was quite evident the bird was dead. What was it like to be dead? He had never seen anything dead before, apart from a snake. And how could anything kill a raven. He had been warned about ravens – to steer clear of them – they could swoop and peck at you and cause you harm, especially to small children. How could there be anything more harmful than a raven that could kill it?

Frank walked back to the truck and the crisp morning air pricked at Damien's bare ankles giving him a shiver propelling him to turn and walk back into the house, back into his room and straight for the window on the inside. The sun had slightly bent its way upwards making the red streak in the window more evident, a scar on the glass pane. He stared at it, not yet dried to brown, its red gave a muted glimmer as the sun hit its paint-like strip as though streaked by an artist's brush.

An eagle killed you. An eagle killed a bird piercing it into a bloody mess. *An eagle made you break your neck.* A wounded raven hurtling like a bombed B52 smashing into a pane of glass. But the glass didn't break. There was no broken glass. The bird was softer than glass. Maybe glass broke the bird, shattering its heart until it was no longer pumping. He wondered whether it had closed its eyes before its fateful fall.

*

"I saw a dead bird today," Damien murmured into the space between him and Ava. He watched as her eyes widened.

"Really?" She gasped with a shudder. "Where?"

"It flew into my window. It died. My grandpa said an eagle probably got it. It was all bloody."

"Urgh," Ava screwed up her face.

"We had to bury it in the garden."

Ava looked on intrigued, as Damien continued.

"Down the back under a tree. I can show you. But here look, you can see where it hit my window. You can see the blood."

Damien stood up from the floor and scooted to the window. He looked behind him motioning Ava to come and she followed. He leaned close to the window sill resting one elbow on its rim and pointed with a free finger at the streak, just visible in the dimming dusk light.

"Look here." He looked at it with her with a certain amazement, at the luck of this small natural catastrophe making its mark within his frame.

Ava stared curiously at the black brown smear. "It must have hit it hard."

"He broke his neck."

"How do you know?"

"It was all floppy like this," Damien flopped his neck askew, his eyes bright with the excitement of his demonstration and poked his tongue out like a thirst ravaged lizard. Ava started to laugh.

"You look like a clown, stupid. Birds don't have tongues." She insisted with a sputtering laugh.

Damien pulled his head back in, along with his tongue. "Don't call me stupid, stupid! You're the clown." He quipped.

"No I'm not."

"Yes you are." He finished.

Ava rolled her eyes at him, "anyway, birds don't have tongues. They have beaks." He squinted his eyes at her as she examined the window in marvel as he wondered himself if she was right or not. He wasn't sure so decided to leave it.

"I haven't seen anything dead before. Except for a snake." Damien turned and plopped himself back on the floor crossing his legs.

Ava turned and looked down at him, resting her back against the wall. "I have seen a snake. But it wasn't dead. I nearly ran over it with my bike." She slid down the wall until she sat on the ground and crossed her legs in front of him, the two of them sitting like natives in their own land around an imaginary fire telling stories of the days of past.

"I nearly trod on one once. They are all through the field."

"The one I nearly rode over was a brown snake. You can die if they bite you."

"I don't think adults die if they are bitten. But children need to stay away from them. My grandpa beats them with the shovel if he sees them." Damien exuded with pride at the chivalry.

"Ah! Frightening! Like spiders."

"The tarantula."

"Have you ever seen one?"

"I saw one at a zoo once."

They sat baking in their own small cocoon of wonder, safely devoid of the insects and reptiles that lurked on the outside of the window and door, the creepers that could sting and bite and kill them. Their chrysalis incubated a hundred creatures of their knowing or intrigue. The spliced black eye that snapped in the eyelid of the kaki cracked skin of an alligator sent a shiver down their spines as Ava recounted one that she saw staring at her once. Then like a soft pawed tiger pup he purred in Ava's ear a dare to outrun him like a leopard. Who was faster to beat? Who was fittest to survive?

"I can run faster than you." She declared.

"No you can't." He rebuffed.

He felt he had already won as soon as she turned the conversation and dipped into the creatures of the deep. She wanted to swim the ocean's deep blue. Damien imagined her swimming in an ocean he had never seen. He had seen it in pictures. He wondered what it must feel like, with never ending water that had no rim. Would it be blue on his skin when he immersed himself underneath?

"The sea is blue because it is a reflection of the sky," Ava said.

Yes, he remembered being told that once. Wondered if it was true.

"Why aren't we blue then?" he asked.

Ava calmly turned her head and looked at the window. "Because it's black outside."

Why aren't we blue then? It's black. It's black. "It's black," Damien stirred as he woke.

CHAPTER TWELVE

Bach Prelude in C major filtered through the room at a slow tempo. It was the first piece of three he had to perform for the eisteddfod. Claudia had dressed him in a white and pale blue striped polo shirt and cream pants and insisted he had his hair cut short back and sides. He sat poised with the very sensation of Mrs White's imaginary taps on his back as he delicately played. It weaved a slumberous tune in the quiet space and Damien disappeared into its sound divorcing himself from the eyes gazing upon him as though no-one else were in the room until his finger pressed upon the final note and lifted off the ivory key. He then sat erect and alert to the attention upon him and nervously turned his head to smile half in knowing he had played it right, half in question was it good enough, only wanting to know *did you hear me play?*

Claudia's eyes brimmed in splendour and Cynthia quietly turned her head to him in a gracious nod thankful that her little boy was turning out alright. He was doing well. *Everything was ok*, she told herself looking at her boy on the stage.

Cynthia took him to the ice cream parlour after it

finished, where Damien clasped his trophy for third place. An act in consolation or for the sake of appearances, it was otherwise recovery of time lost, ignoring the lengthy gaps.

"That was very good," Cynthia placated as she reached her hand out to brush the hair on his forehead out of his eyes gently resting it like a lick of a tongue.

It was an endorsement that rang in Damien's ears as he led the way into the parlour taking a booth for the three of them.

"You keep your practice up and you'll have first place in no time." Cynthia nodded at him encouragingly whereupon Damien shrugged his shoulders nodding in vigour.

"What flavour would you like?" Claudia prodded.

"Cookies and cream," Damien submitted.

"With extra cream?"

Damien nodded "extra cream and a cherry." He flicked back as he mussed the cow lick out of the top of his head.

Damien smiled. *She* was smiling at him. He could sense her cautious eyes, but he couldn't be happier. She was playing with him. The bright lights of the parlour, its fresh cream walls and candied embellishments made the place seem like a box of sweets that made Damien want to stay for as long as possible devouring each sensational bite and suck down their syrup making him giddy with pleasure. This is the way life should be, he thought. In this moment. This is the way he wanted it to be. This is the way it was before when it was just the three of them.

He licked down the spoon as he scooped up the cream and cracked pieces of dough, lapping at the vanilla sweetness between the chunks of chocolate crunch. In the auditorium he was able to drown out everything around him as he played, from the euphoria it created. The feeling hadn't left him as he drowned out the sound of voices around him, conversations not requiring his ears, as he swirled the cream in his mouth closing his eyes. He just wanted to be.

A bitter aroma impregnated him. He opened his eyes and looked at the cups with the liquorice liquid sitting in front of them. Its scent took him away from the flavours in his mouth. Was it the cup in front of Claudia? No, she was drinking tea. It wasn't the scent of leaves that he could smell. He turned to look at the other opposite him. That was the one with pungency. Hers. A smell that reminded him of that first fateful day she took him out on the weekend. *That* weekend. The weekend that equalled the box on the floor he'd left by the door. The box now unloaded. The weekend she had been sipping a cup of coffee when she took him out for a milkshake. He saw her look at her watch. Both seemed obsessed with their watch. Watches were time. Time to go home. But not with her. The ice cream started to taste too sweet. Maybe he shouldn't have asked for the extra cream. Or was it the cherry? It made his stomach churn and he wanted to vomit.

He wondered whether he should tell them he wanted to be sick. He looked up at Cynthia in front of him, then at Claudia as his eyes became alert to the waitress standing beside the next table. Who should he tell? He didn't want to tell them at all, for fear they would think he was weak. A strange twinging sweetness sensed at the back of his throat, he looked up at them both in wanton horror. Cynthia looked at him in the face with concern.

"Are you alright? You have suddenly gone pale." She stretched her hand out to his head and wiped the top of his forehead.

"I need to be sick." He mumbled.

Cynthia scuffed out the edge of the seat and grabbed Damien by the arm and ran with him down the back to the bathroom, where he launched the entire contents of his stomach into the toilet bowl. She rubbed him on his back.

He grimaced sitting back on his knees, a pale shade of teal.

Cynthia gave a tired sigh, "dearie me, eyes bigger than your stomach. That's what that is, isn't it?" She tried to placate. "Come on then." She walked with him to the basin supporting his gangly frame where she wetted her handkerchief under the tap. "Here," she reached over and wiped his face, Damien pleased at its cooling sensation, before handing him the cloth to hold to his face as she tucked his shirt back into his pants.

"You'll be ok. We had better get you home."

The two of them walked back into the parlour to where Claudia was still sitting apprehensively in the corner of the booth. Upon seeing the concerned look on Claudia's face, even in his half daze, Damien felt like wanting to squirm away in humiliation.

"You ok?"

He nodded with as much candour as physically reachable.

"Time to go home." Cynthia dead-panned.

His trophy sat lopsided along the vinyl booth seat, forlorn without its owner. Damien reached in to grab it as they started to head toward the door. The treacle trimmings of the creamery lent a new distinct rancour in which he'd be happy to never return.

Claudia dropped Cynthia off first. She lived nearby. An old high school friend had been looking after Rory for the day. It was clear Cynthia was anxious to get back.

"You should be proud," she turned to Damien as she got out of the car. "Bye sweetheart."

Damien watched as she walked up to the front door of her house. It was plain and unadorned. There was a small rose bush fraying wildly at the edge of the veranda leading up to it.

He looked on waiting for her to turn around and wave goodbye. She pulled out her keys and put them in the front door and went inside. As the car moved with the forward thrust of acceleration, he turned his head back, thinking maybe she would pop outside again, because she had just wanted to drop her handbag inside before waving him goodbye.

Claudia drove off down the main road to take him home. The car bumped along with Damien in the backseat with the empty seat beside him. The seat's dark caramel velveteen covers were not like the nylon in the back seat of his mother's car that were covered in the stains of children. He didn't know which ones he preferred.

There was something about those marks. Some of those marks were his. Even after a slam of the door after an exit, she'd be carrying him with her everywhere.

*

The sick feeling continued to lurk in his stomach as he lay in bed. He stared into the dusky black of the room, trying to focus on something. Anything. His stomach swirled with a butterfly nest making a see-saw sensation, or was it bees biting inside of him, frantic and alarmed. A hot sticky sweat slapped him, slamming him oddly cold. He pulled up the covers. Finally, his eyes caught a small glimmer coming from the edges of the trophy he had won, briefly illuminated by light from outside as it sat on the shelf at the other end of the room. He stared at it, trying to make out its form. He hurriedly pulled down the sheets and scurried to pick it up off the shelf and pulled it with him back into bed, deftly propping it on his pillow beside him, tucking it in with the sheet.

He rolled his head to the side as he lay on the pillow, staring at the trophy's golden flanks. He re-imagined how he had played, could see all the people who had occupied seats in the auditorium that he had only allowed as a glimpse. Their vicinity was now a million miles away and his capacity to be in front of so many seemed infinite. Slowly the sensations in his stomach started to disappear. He patted the square mahogany edge of the trophy's bust as though it were a shoulder and muttered to it "Good job."

He sighed and let out small tufts of breath as he stared beyond the trophy to the window, seeing the distant speck-like stars with their glossy pebble eyes winking. Maybe tomorrow she might surprise him and come and pick him up because he had been sick. Finish the day as it had started. Happy. *Maybe tomorrow she will take me to her house.* It was a new house she had moved into. He had never seen what it was like inside. Wondered where her room was. Where Rory's was. Where they slept. Wondered where his room was, he was sure there was a room for him, she just hadn't gotten it ready yet. The place looked big enough from the outside. It was a whole house. He closed his eyes thinking of what the next day might bring. Thinking of the next day lulled him into sleep.

*

The next day came and the next day went, seemingly quicker than the honeyed maple leaf that he watched fall and flutter to the ground as he sat outside the door on the front veranda. He had picked at some dandelions that burst from the side of the step through its cracks, twilling them round in his hands tearing them apart until they made his fingers stink.

No-one came. Not that anyone said they would. He walked back into the house as the night fell. Claudia had cooked lamb chops and potato mash with ketchup for dinner. It was his favourite. But meal times now started to take on a strange turn, as he picked at the food not feeling hungry. The lamb was like soggy cardboard in his mouth, making it hard to swallow. And the two people opposite him seemed like strangers and he an uninvited guest in a house that was not his. They silently ate, with the subtle clank of sliding cutlery and the creak of his chair the only inhibition in the room. From his throat to the pit of his stomach he felt a hole, a deep cavernous space inflaming. Claudia with her ordinariness and Frank with his calm, their faces directed on their plates as their mouths macerated their food in a pantomime made for a visceral inertia of the solitary housed within his gut. He excused himself from the table and walked to his bedroom.

The room was as quiet as the one he had left and was empty except for the props of his bed, a desk, his closet and drawers, assembled around a perimeter with the stage of isolation hollow in its centre. There was nowhere he could hide between them other than beneath his bed. His eyes furtively glanced in a desperation that exhausted itself upon trying and the only space was the one that was exposed, the one where he dropped to the floor with his legs crossed and put his hands to his head. The silence grazed his ears like the serrated leaves of a Himalayan birch.

He reached under the bed and pulled out his keyboard and thrashed away on it mercilessly with the sound on mute. No sound was better than anything that may invite attention into the room. The longer he bashed at it, the more illuminated the keys rang out their imaginary sound. Imaginary as the place they helped him to go – someplace other than where he was. He eventually slowed their pace as it calmed, like floating on a boat set out to sea. He knew how to make peace with the rapids in which he'd been flung - the rapids of hoping, wishing and dreaming of something that always seemed to elude him - but he hoped he wouldn't fly down that same river again. He hit the last key. It was enough.

CHAPTER THIRTEEN

The hessian sack scratched like mites crawling inside it biting at his skin. The teacher had dressed him and a few others in the sacks wrapped by belts of twine as they lined up in their positions at the back rehearsing the nativity scene. Damien and Patrick were selected to be shepherds. They didn't have to say anything, just be present. He was as equally content by this as he was slightly perturbed by it. Claudia was in the middle of making his outfit. He patiently had his measurements taken the preceding afternoon and watched her start cutting out the calico.

A boy called Brett was chosen to play Joseph. He was good at talking. Damien was not. And a girl called Felicity played Mary. She was cute and pretty and she liked talking too. But she never talked to Damien. She used to sit and giggle in a group with other girls. That's when Patrick caught his attention as a tactic of diversion as they stood there awaiting instruction. He bloated out the hessian sack in front of his belly mimicking a waddle on the spot as Felicity made her entrance hobbling with her faux pregnant bump.

Damien giggled. Then somebody broke wind and they both started laughing.

Felicity leaned on Brett's arm, he awkward in his hold of his second-grade class mate. The tan plastic baby suddenly materialised by the third act thanks to the stilted efforts of Rodney who shuffled a wooden crib on the stage, almost toppling it over leaving baby Jesus exposed, swaddling flying free.

Damien had become sufficiently aware of where babies came from. From the bellies of mothers. He knew where Rory came from - had watched curiously as his mother's shape had grown until he had seen her go back to normal again - some time later, after disappearing. But he didn't know how a baby got in there or how it got out. They were apparently a gift from God. That is how Claudia explained it to him, how she had explained where Rory came from. "Just like you," she had told him. But that is as far as it extended. It was Patrick who explained the rest - in great detail.

And it was how their play started to turn into jokes about anatomy and what each meant to the other and how magnetically repulsive they were and how positively lewd and disgusting the thought of having their privates anywhere near a girl's.

It had made him start to grow coy about being naked in front of his grandmother. She was the one who always ran his bath and sat there on a stool beside him washing his hair, occasionally walking out to let him be for a few minutes playing in the water. Now he started to cover himself up with the wash cloth hovering it above his legs in the bath, until one day he told her he was ok and she could go. From there on in, she let him be. As soon as she was out and the door closed behind her, he lifted the wash cloth and gazed at the small pale pink crumpled skin protruding between his legs. He'd pluck at it watching it bobble like a fat lazy worm beneath the water. It seemed a useless extension growing out of him and couldn't imagine it disappearing inside of someone else, inside of a girl – why anyone would want to put one where Patrick said it went he didn't really know. *To make babies.* He decided he didn't like babies and therefore didn't need to pursue something that he believed Patrick made up anyway.

It gave him a desperate urge to ask Ava. Maybe she knew something he didn't, could correct Patrick's incorrect information. But it was usually Ava who asked all the questions. Somehow he didn't want to stifle the air between them with petty absurdities. He scoffed at the idea. It wasn't for discussion with a girl. What would she know anyway? He knew more than she did. Maybe he should ask John he had thought. He relented not to bring it up with anyone at all.

The thought of bodies, a girl's and a boy's made him feel awkward as he sat in his room where the days were starkly short as they closed themselves black and the ice that bathed the house made it harder to go outside, leaving him with too much time to think of each new fact of life that came flooding in. And fewer people around to ask. The snow brought the mud of containment and exclusion. He saw his mother less. And Frank only took extra trips into the town when he had a dire need. The sky was mottled grey until it went swarthy as though on the verge of tears. The colour of mourning. And when the rain fell as sleet it bit with a stinging frost that left him frozen.

Christmas Day had come and gone without the present he had wanted. He pulled the woollen sweater she had given him on the day out of the closet. It was blue with green flecks through it which she knitted for him, which meant her hands had touched it everywhere. He put it on and hugged himself in it. Maybe next Christmas she would give him what he wanted. Her invitation.

He pulled it off and discarded it on the floor by his bed. A year was a long time to wait. It made the snowman he had built with Rory out front melt away its false protuberance leaving the coal black eyes its only evidence, something tangible in its memory.

*

Cold mornings pathed the way to warm afternoons with Mrs White. Her house was a cloister of blood red cushions and gold tasseled drapes and smelt like maple pancakes. The piano where they played had a mustiness to it that smelt worn but welcoming for its long habitation. It was the scent of familiarity, as was her faded Miss Dior perfume.

Three years down the line and Mrs White's enthusiasm had only grown with Damien as he progressed advancing through the fourth syllabus a year ahead. She'd brought her turntable out and started playing records whereby she taught him how to play along with them in tempo. He attempted the same exercise at home. Frank had a turntable where he spun records whenever the mood conveyed, hurling out Henry Mancini and Frank Sinatra. Damien found a Mozart prelude in the record stash that Mrs White had taught him from which he knew he could play. It reinvented his Sunday afternoons from the contained solo piano into a resounding echo of accompaniment.

Claudia often sat on the sofa in the living room listening to him play as he practised every afternoon. She was his humble confidant in a conversation of his musical aptitude, not through any words expressed, only from her physical presence. She exhibited a patience like no other and helped him by re-setting the needle on the turntable back to start from the beginning, happy to listen to him replay the same pieces several times through.

It all changed forever when John gave him his own

turntable and a single. A Starman[5] entered the room.

He spent hours transfixed by the spinning wheel, watching the shiny black disc with its grooves shriek out its crackling hiss and propel into the room its song. Over and over he played it. He learnt all the words, but the best part was when he lay on his back and hummed along. John had played it for him in the car one day. It was when he was in front of it on his own in his room that the vinyl scraped out a breath that was an air for his own breathing. It was intoxicating.

He knew he could replicate it, and he played by ear picking it up on the keyboard. Now the possibilities of what he could do appeared infinite. Infinite as the sky. Infinite as the stars in the song. He lay on his back on his bed and leaned his head upwards, where he could see out the window and stare up at the stars. They all seemed so far away from where he was. He wondered whether their sparkle was really the tail lights of spaceships, whether there were people up there, out there. Did they know he was down here? Maybe they could see everything. Maybe they knew everything. Maybe they could see what was happening to him. Because no one on earth had a clue.

He'd roll over, reach out and gently place the needle back to the outer rim and let it slide into its swirl of tune as he lay back on his bed as it whirled in his brain.

He placed the vinyl back in its sleeve and tucked the turntable under the bed. Sitting in his pyjamas on the bed, he replayed the song's pre-chorus on his keyboard. It rung out its electric tone like a chime in a cave. Its retinue was always an amiable one. One where Ava sat and watched cross legged in front of him.

---

[5] Bowie, David. "Starman" from *The Rise and Fall of Ziggy Stardust and the Spiders from Mars*. Performed by David Bowie. RCA Records. 1972.

"See, I can copy it," he told her. He played it for her again.

"It sounds like those buttons you push playing pinball," she suggested.

"Well, sort of, but not really. This is heaps better."

"It jingles."

"Like bells."

"But not like Christmas." She smirked.

"Like snowflakes hitting the window," he smiled at her.

CHAPTER FOURTEEN

"That ought to do it," Frank pulled the bike upright from the bench in the shed and placed it back on the ground. He had rewound a new tread on the tyre after Damien had popped it one afternoon during a late afternoon skidding session down the side road from a paddock. He had stacked the bike slewing it through the dirt, leaving a bloody smear as he grazed his elbow and knee. The slip was never going to be enough to defy him from the bike's ultimate assurance of his freedom. With the bike he could go everywhere.

He knew every back road, every lane and every path that it tolerated without getting stuck in the mud. He slashed through streams traipsing from one hard bank to the next and through into adjacent fields rampant with green shoots or pale lime taloned crops. He could ride as far as Patrick's house and the two met up and rode up and down the long drives of neighbours kicking back as much dust in dry dirt or fleck each other with the splashback of mud. The dirtier they got, the more evidence of a ride worth the making. Until he made it home and Claudia locked it in the shed in the hope he would learn not to make such a mess.

"Keep out of the dirt," she had firmly instructed him. She

had crankily grabbed his arm the day he had grazed it pulling his elbow round into view so he could see what he had done, the red gash encrusted with grit. "See what happens!"

Damien had decided he didn't particularly care. The pain of its sting felt good. It reminded him he was awake and still breathing - that he existed. Its mark evidence of the rigour of the fall.

While the bike was locked up he derived an equal amount of pleasure in walking as far away from the house as he could and had started collecting cicadas' skins. He'd pluck them up careful not to crack their caramel parchment membranes. Now that the winter and spring had passed and the ground once hard now cracked itself open, he'd hunt down the back field finding the holes from which their bodies had lain their absent casing. He had crammed an empty container full of them late one afternoon after a week-long haul. On his walk back to the house he topped each fence post with one like an ornament. If they had lit up after completing his path they would have looked like glow worms guarding from their fort-wood stakes. They were his army and his protection.

One of his commanders had toppled. He struck a light from a stolen box of matches and lit him up lying in the dirt, watching it crackle and burst apart. It gave off a rank odour as he became mesmerized by the glow left in its wake. He'd find another one to replace him at some point.

Once Damien had retrieved his bike after a week-long banishment, he rode over to Patrick's. Patrick had a long concrete driveway down the side of his house, where the two of them ripped their SSP racers. Both of them had the added benefit of having the Smash-Up Derby box set. With multiple ramps and cars they ripped the cords through the chassis and spun their wheels with a cataclysmic speed smashing them into the brick wall of the house scattering the hoods, doors and trunks apart with tyres whirling asunder.

After a round of obliteration he picked up the debris of their cars and snapped them back together. He took Patrick's car to relaunch a kamikaze speedster, with a demonic tail wind until it crashed into the wall, leaving a smear.

"Ah! Ha! Ha!" Patrick laughed until he picked up the pieces. "Wow. It's hot."

Damien walked over and inspected the damage, could feel the heat when he plucked up a part. The boot had cracked its plastic body. He was nevertheless impressed. Except it was an attempt not to be tried again, especially after Mrs Arncliffe poked her head around the side of the house to ask what they were doing. These toys were a precious commodity that he did not want to risk losing.

"Well, I guess I'll see you tomorrow then," Damien placed the plastic and metal back into Patrick's hands and collected up his own car shoving the set in a plastic bag.

"Yeah." Patrick surrendered. "I think my set is broken." He looked at the parts in his hands despondently.

Damien looked at the pieces in Patrick's hands. "Nah, nothing breaks in this set. Here give it to me." Patrick handed them back over. Damien took the car door and bonnet and snapped them back in, after some heavy shoving. "See, it's sort of alright."

It was wonky and askew, but nevertheless satisfied Damien, until he handed it back to Patrick who could tell the door wouldn't close properly. Damien just shrugged his shoulders. Patrick had to accept what he was given, forever the humble servant to Damien's state of play.

"See you," Patrick waved as Damien mounted his bike and twirled it down the driveway in the direction of home, with a stoicism forgoing any sense of liability.

Patrick watched his friend ride off, accepting of the dregs at his feet. He picked up the pieces of what Damien had left.

He told himself it was ok. He liked being with him. He made him laugh and always had a head full of ideas which always created one too many adventures too hard to ignore their challenge. Back in the classroom they were on equal terms. You got things right or you got them wrong and the rewards or punishments would be the same. School was a test that was a different kind of game, played only by the rules that they both had to follow equally. Outside of it, Damien had his own that Patrick had to fit. It was just a toy anyway and Patrick hadn't stopped him.

Back home Damien sat on the end of the veranda. From a box of Redheads he struck a light one after the other and flicked them off into the distance. With each stroke he watched the flame swing back toward him on its departure then haphazardly scatter and disperse as though quenched by a mist of water. He was mesmerized by the way the fire erupted from an angry burst out of nowhere, then almost disappointed it went out so quickly. He jumped off the edge of the veranda and collected all the little white sticks he had flicked and arranged them all as a little tepee on the grass, a house he made out of the things he had burned. The flame of a warm place left charcoal black, yet the little conical home at his feet had the strength of its structure from the white of its base. The charcoal was what crumbled. Its roof. The part used to console the child. *I fed you and clothed you and put a roof over your head*. It was warped. Push it hard enough and it would fall in. When he looked up it was missing.

There was always going to be missing pieces everywhere he looked, the knowledge unconsciously harbouring somewhere in his brain. The missing things rattled him more than the things that were there. So many missing things that equated to nothing. Why did a sense of nothing pound so hard at him? Warp and destroy. It was useless attaching to something that was going to be gone at some point anyway.

That's when you threw them away. He put the matches back in his pocket.

CHAPTER FIFTEEN

There was a terrible storm that had closed the door on that summer. Like the fluttering shutters of a decrepit bar that rapidly flapped from a chaotic turbine breeze unhinging and extracting them from their crux. And it was Ava who had been at its pivot the night that the storm came through, the moment the clouds brought their shadow and the wind scattered dust into a haze like phantoms breathing out a toxic plume.

"Where is your mother?" She asked, with a delicate innocence.

He was taken aback by her question. He looked at her briefly at her curious eyes. He could tell she really wanted to know. He looked at the floor, embarrassed.

"She is in town."

"Why aren't you?" She asked with unadorned inquiry.

It was a simple question. Three words. He knew how to answer most things. This one he didn't know how. He looked up and stared off into space. The space of the black outside the window. There outside, amid the chaos of frightened trees clutching into the earth there was no chaos compared to the question a whirr in his head. There in the black there was nothing. There was no obfuscation. There in the black his mind could be calm. His eyes drifted down to the jar of pebbles sitting on the sill. The jar he had used to drop off his collection to contain the round rocky forms after each trip back from the brook. If an answer equalled a pebble then there would be nearly twenty four answers now from which he could pick. He tried his best at one.

"I don't know."

Damien looked up at her and nodded his head, in acknowledgement of the answer he chose.

"It won't be forever. That's what they said."

The window rattled as a burst of wind gust battered it reverberating in a shiver knocking the jar on the sill to the floor. The glass splintered apart on the hardwood and the pebbles scattered their bobbling forms. Like marbles racing across slats. Ava shuddered at the sound and jerked as the splatter of glass and stone debris cut in front of her. Damien winced as a splinter of glass grazed him. He looked down to see a trickle of blood from above his knee as he stood in fright.

Claudia opened the door and skirted into the room. "What's happened in here?" She cried out. "That was a horrible noise." She looked to the centre of the room with Damien standing in a puddle of broken glass and pebbles, and a line of blood to his ankle. "Oh dear," she delicately took his hand, "be careful, tread over this way," she pulled at him as he carefully followed her instruction.

"It's ok, it was just a jar that fell down from the window." Damien asserted as to the cacophony.

"Oh look, you're bleeding." She said in anxious haste. "Why did you put it up there for?"

"I'm sorry." He held back tears which caused a pain so intense in the back of his throat he couldn't breathe in. He felt like he was in trouble for something that wasn't his fault. He didn't make the jar of stinking pebbles crash. It was God. The God that made him made the pebbles crash. What could he do to convince his grandmother that it wasn't his fault? He wasn't to blame. It was the God that made him who was to blame. God made the pebbles crash.

Or maybe it was Ava.

No. It was his fault. He had lied and God got angry. Because he *did* know.

An anger somehow seemed to transpose down and into him. The pain in his throat turned into a pain in his chest, like a rapid-fire thud that wanted to beat outward and hit something. He wished the jar was back on the sill so he could repeat its action. He wanted to pick it up and bash it down hard onto the floor. He could stomp on it with his legs like a jackhammer not caring that the soles of his shoes would be thorned by shards of glass.

Claudia took him to the bathroom where she cleaned his cut making it look worse with the brown of iodine. The quiet of the space only invited more noise to swamp his head with all the words he wanted to say. There were too many crammed inside, too many things he wanted to say, but wasn't allowed to. He tried to open his mouth and nothing came out as he tried to say *it wasn't my fault.*

He stared at the neat line of Claudia's hair along the tip of her forehead as her head bent down in careful attention as he sat on the edge of the tub. She had a stress frown between her brows that left a permanent mark through time. He hadn't noticed it until now. Then she looked up at him after she pasted down the edges of a plaster.

"There we are." She soothed, softly slapping the side of his thigh. There was something in the hazel green of her eyes that made him stare longer than he had or had ever noticed of them before. They were the eyes of origin of how he came to be, the eyes of her daughter, a reminder. He tried to picture the whole of his mother's face in her place. But wishful thinking was just that, and he didn't want to turn his mind upside down on account of a person who wasn't even there.

He crept back to his room, where he could hear Frank sweeping the remnants of glass and pebbles into a dustpan. Some of them had split apart revealing their interior, a wave of colour like the rings of a sawn tree. As Frank walked to the bin, Damien quickly followed and plucked up a pebble in haste before he threw them all away. Maybe he would keep just the one. He felt the whole of it in his hand as he walked back to his room. He put it back on the windowsill despite the catastrophe it had caused. It was now free of the jar that had contained it, its true catastrophe. The sill was a place for his prized possessions. The window was the only visible place of escape, and they'd be the only things he'd want to take with him when the day came, the day when he'd get away.

CHAPTER SIXTEEN

It was a perfect quadrant, the way the black metal hand with its stalk-like wrist and curlicue ends pointed at nine with the other resting half way around its globe. Hours, minutes that turned into days then weeks before overlapping themselves into months, then years. The time struck, not with the chime of a bell but with the beat of its longitude. It wasn't on the hour, but on the half way point – an odd position for its drawing attention to his gaze. Nine and a half years he could count for every half inch he could measure as its hands shifted from each point around the clock.

"I'm in town now love, I'll see you more often." Those were the words she had said – a long time ago. It had been over three years since she had first gone off – off into her own land of oblivion, without him. He was tired. He was irritated by a promise that revealed little. She had seen him, alright, but she didn't let him come home. The time had now come. He had had enough of her perpetual bait.

"Why can't I come home with you?" Damien dared one afternoon close to Christmas. There was a chill in the air, the snow had started to fall. The pine trees glared their heavy trench coats which skirted the road as he sat in the back seat of her car as she drove him back home to Claudia and Frank's.

"No Damien. We've made arrangements." She mumbled sternly.

"Why didn't you come get me? I didn't know where you went. Why did you leave me there?" He burst into tears angry with heated breath. It wasn't good enough.

She slipped out something inaudible. Then she said nothing and just drove on. His tears stained his eyes into a hazy blur. The pine trees rattled and gnashed their needles. If they had mouths he was sure they'd bite. It was the ice that would sting, deep into his veins if they managed to cut through his skin. Sleet sliced across the pane as frozen as the tears on his cheeks.

The ride home grew bleak. Darkness swallowed the cool grey sun turning it to dusk and the space between the house and the car never looked so inviting – the hearth looked like a welcome mat to paradise compared to the car he ran out of, slamming the door behind him, shutting it in her face.

Claudia walked out wondering what all the racket was about as Damien watched her approach the car, Cynthia standing outside of it, leftover tears on her cheeks. She seemed to crumple in on herself as Claudia approached her. He turned back around and walked heavy footed in through the doorway and didn't look back.

Three and a half years to figure out that that was that. That there was no invitation, that there was never going to be one. There was no homecoming, there was to be no Damien in Cynthia's home. She liked other children better. She liked Rory better. Better than him. The baby. The baby with its marble eyes and pudgy face. The baby that comes from the belly of mothers. Babies - he loathed - like the mother who bore it. And anything she had ever said was as vacant as the heart housed in her body, vacant as the house in which she lived, the one he was never going to be in.

Winter had a new name. It was the name of the skipped seasons, the ones that he couldn't remember occurring since the winter that preceded this. The winter of one long year. Where all the decorations of occasions seemed muted and worn as though they never happened. Bows and fairy floss – that had gone mouldy. Stuck in a room with a window and a door where he could no longer run and only imagine the field where his legs could take him. A field adorned with bluebells that turned into snapdragons that bit, like a frost bite of a pine needle wedged in white. The soft cotton white of the snow with a glorious radiant sun was the fraud of the season – the sun made it melt into stone. If you slipped and fell you could break your body to pieces.

That's when it started. Damien had started to feel incorporeal. Weightless. Disembodied. As though he wasn't there, here or anywhere. His body had escaped itself, too difficult to reconcile it with the hardwood floor, his reality of the foundation upon which he stood. Like the bottle cap scratched upon crumbled concrete, he felt like he was part cap, scratched and chipped, part concrete disintegrated. But he couldn't be that if he was pulsating human flesh. A boy. A boy that God had made. *Then God why are you doing this to me?*

Noise. Too much noise in the containment of four walls. In a room where he couldn't move. A room where he couldn't feel.

He turned on the transistor radio by his bed. Bloody Mary Morning[6] shunted through the room while he swung Dark Side of The Moon onto his turntable and let it overlap its tune furling like an angry wave, amorphous in the room, as he pulled out his keyboard and struck his fingers rampant upon its keys. A cacophony. Volume. Max peak.

---

[6] Nelson, Willie. "Bloody Mary Morning" from *Phases and Stages*. Performed by Willie Nelson. Atlantic. 1974.

A clash of a hundred keys bounced in an echo, ridding the room of its claustrophobic emptiness where notes scattered and tumbled around him like waves at the mouth of a shell. This was his shell where his ears leant themselves to the reverberations of an ocean. Maybe like Ava's ocean. The sound was his ocean. One where he could swim, where his body was his again. He was buoyant. There was no need for a floor upon which to stand. He knew how to create his own way of being, where all the parts could put themselves back together again.

He looked down at his arm and at his hand as he stopped still. He wiped the wetness from his face with the back of his hand. He could feel it. He existed. He was himself. The turntable scratched out its silent end. The Who were left playing on the radio.

Claudia gently pushed open his door.

CHAPTER SEVENTEEN

Between two bars on a staff, there was a point where there would always be a rest, whole or quartered, a line struck as in sand. He couldn't keep bashing out the same tune. In the moments of quietude he tried his best at furrowing into books, wedging himself on the seat in the living room, closest to the window catching some sun. He tried steeping himself into the world of Robin Hood and King Arthur. He knew the forest of green in which Robin snuck through like an outlaw, where he could imagine himself running. And there in his forest were the same stones, like the ones at the brook where Arthur exhibited his strength. But how could he ever have the strength of the great Knight to pull out the sword. How was it possible? He imagined the arms of a man, a million miles away in his own image, protruding muscular forms, the glazed and rippling taut muscle of a galloping stallion, a black glossy beauty. To him it was a comparison for which he felt physically impotent, a boy with a small and wiry frame. Weak. What was it like to be a man? Is that what a man was, muscular and chivalrous, a bandit and a fighter?

He noticed the older boys at school more often than he ever had before. They seemed to grow beyond him. It made him conscious of their superior forms. He watched them collect on the field as he waited for the afternoon bus. Boys in shorts running the oval; or boys in strapped down whites waging a game with a ball. He was curious to the nature of their preparation and play, wondered if he could be like them, extend into the capabilities of what they could do.

He grabbed the bat from Patrick as they took turns at junior baseball trials that had started in the spring. Damien was small and lithe, but he was incredibly nimble. He wasn't born for sport and felt less so as he watched a few of his classmates sprint their gazelle-like bodies from base to base. He preferred the feel of an instrument between his hands rather than the thick metal baseball bat that vibrated with pain when he hit with it, not resonance like the baton of a drum. When he launched the ball, however, that's when he could hit the ground running like a terrier bullish in its haste. Damien was remarkably fast. And competitive. He got what he wanted. He got into the team. He wanted to prove it and nothing could stop him now that he had.

Every afternoon was now occupied with as much as he could afford - piano lessons once a week, school orchestra twice, then baseball practise on a Friday afternoon. They played the game on Saturday. He sang the choir on Sunday. All his bases covered. Music and sweat of a boy going on ten. Stagnant time was silence and here he had no silence voraciously occupying every minute. Every minute gave him a thirst for more to prove that he could do it all.

Patrick's father picked the two boys up some Friday afternoons in order to watch the end of their practise. One game day Saturday Damien had outpaced the pitcher's final catch and scored a home run. He was good as a pitcher during practice, but when it came to a game, he was a hitter, delivering an oblique ball trajectory confounding his fielders, then whipping a thoroughbred run. He liked being in the batter's box. It was a concoction of control versus none. A frightened anticipation as you stood there waiting for a velocity unknown, swiftly followed by the power of the juddering bash of the hit. Except it wasn't over, there was more to come – you had to run.

"You hit that ball like Hammerin Hank! How'd you learn that?" Patrick's father boasted as he walked up to him in the outfield after the game was done.

Damien smiled at him and shrugged his shoulders. He didn't need to say anything.

"We'll get you in the Centre Field. Like Joe D." Patrick's father enthused as he drove him home.

"Did you know he is Mr Coffee® on tv?" Patrick digressed. The boys in the team all knew Joe, the famous baseball player who sold coffee machines. A boy in the team brought a magazine ad to the practise session to reveal the celebrity of their newly chosen sport. Damien had seen him on television.

"That's right, Mr Coffee. Selling like hotcakes."

Reconciling the older grey haired man he had seen on the television with the legend of athletic prowess was unequal. As though something had become altered in the way in which the man ought to be, to stay. Is that what happened to man? The concept of youth and its placement in life he did not understand. Like looking at two separate people – whereby Damien was the third-party onlooker yet to enter stage one of manhood.

Merle Haggard was playing on the deck in the dash. Patrick's father softly tapped his fingers on the steering wheel as Damien stared out the window.

"I was almost only going to be a mid-fielder." Damien cast out dissatisfied.

"Oh yeah? What's so bad about that?"

"Well, you don't do anything." Damien shifted awkwardly in the seat.

Patrick's father raised his brow.

"You just stand there." Damien quipped.

"You watch and you catch." Patrick's father merged a thought through the discourse.

"Hmm." He calculated it in his brain.

"You catch to collect a win."

He ran his mind over the comment, but he remained unconvinced. He still liked to hit. To hit and run.

Weeks passed and the season was chasing itself to close. Friday afternoon practise and Saturdays' games seemed less tantalising with the frequency of riding his bike home by himself. He had thought he saw Cynthia standing off by the cyclone fence in the distance one of the days, on its other side, restricted, not permitted. By the time he turned around again there was no-one there. She'd bought him a baseball when he signed up for the trials. It was pricier than most. He knew she couldn't afford such extravagances, she was always telling him she couldn't afford things. He didn't know if it was some sort of consolation gift in lieu of all those tears that day. She'd treaded gently around him ever since. His grandpa Frank was often his only mascot.

He had spent hours in the backyard practising with the ball and launch prop, dizzying in his effort with the number of times he raced to collect each ball he hit, to place it back in position and hit it off its mantel. Who was he hitting the ball for? It leant him into a state aggrieved in its solipsism. Until he returned with his team, the only ones left to impress.

It was the second last game of the season and Damien was waiting in the bullpen with three other boys. His coach had stepped out over the other side of the field. His number was called to the pitch, due to be next. As soon as he stood, Rick from his team stood up and shoved Damien to the side wanting to go ahead. Rick towered a foot taller, his height a clobbering sole of a shoe in his face. Damien was no match. He tried to shove back. Rick shoved him harder skirting him back on the bench and walked onto the field. Damien stood up sniggering in disbelief. *It was my turn.* He fumed.

By the time he got the call, the spark that had ignited the fuse only blew up a stature stomped upon. He fouled every ball. He walked off despondent, crushed. Then the coach didn't pick him to bat.

"You did alright out there?" Frank put forth unconsciously soliciting a response.

"Ah, no, not really. I fouled." Damien expelled his breath in a haphazard form of low.

"You had a go Damien, that's all that matters." Frank patted him on the back encouragingly.

"Yeah, I guess."

"It means you have more to make up for next time. Keep practising." Frank opened the door of the truck.

Frank's easy demeanour had a way that settled without force or abundance. But that was as far as the conversation went. Damien wanted to tell him about Rick and what he did. That what he did was wrong. He hadn't stuck by the order of things. He hadn't stuck by the rules. He had been next. But the breadth of the silence in the cab made the words clump in the back of his throat like lead. The moment had passed. Damien just stayed angry. He was stuck in an incapacity to reveal and tell. If life was to have an order of things, then why should they not be in his favour? To verbalise such a question into open air was impossible like the sapped-up hole in a tree. So all his questions remained unanswered. The order of things in baseball seemed to be stacked against him. By the time he was back in his room he decided he no longer liked the sport or his team or any boy in it. He was sure they wouldn't want him back anyway. He would know by next Friday. He would know then, because his coach could tell him if he didn't want him in the team anymore. He felt a sickening twinge in his gut. He was sure his gut was right.

He went into the living room and pulled out his piano book and set it up on the cradle, opening the lid as he sat himself on the stool. He practised his scales, then played the entire book he had opened from beginning to end, then replayed again a second time through without needing to look. This is where he felt safe. This is what he knew. This is what he could control in whatever direction and order of his choosing. He closed the book in front of him and placed his fingers on the keys and allowed a caterpillar dance upon them until they slunk into a melody that usurped his throne and returned the sense of wellbeing.

"That's a nice one Damien. What one is that?" Claudia mentioned in passing.

"I just made it up," he said nonchalantly.

"Oh, well best write it down then," she ducked her head back in the room, "catch it while you have it."

He thought it an odd thing to say. No-one, not even Mrs White had expressed such a phrase for action – he had never played her anything of his own creation. But he was like a butterfly catcher without his net. It had already escaped him, he couldn't remember what he had just played. It didn't matter. They were just notes vociferously parrying from his fingertips into the air, ridding the tension congested in his chest from the breath of defeat. But here he had now won without even trying. Order restored. Maybe he should ask her to buy him some paper. It was a question he was capable of and one he knew she should be able to afford.

*

Claudia had bought him the paper at his request. She took him for a special trip the Monday after school to Edgar's Music Store in town. G Schirmer® Royal Brand manuscript, authentic, stamped. These were his, not the pre-filled music books of Mrs White's, as he carried them under his arm walking out of the store. As soon as he was home, he peeled the pages open like a mango skin, exposing an exotic fruit he had never tasted, their blank pages revealing something he was yet to know. The blank stave, something he was ravenous to fill.

He lay on his stomach in the middle of his bedroom floor, kicking his legs back behind him, keyboard in front of him and his clean book of sheets to his side. He'd play a collection of notes, then with his lead pencil, drew their stick figure hieroglyphs on the page. As Damien drew treble clefs, Ava doodled flowers all around the edge.

"See, it's actually not that hard if you put your mind to it," he said.

"I suppose so," she happy in her own pursuits. "What are you making anyway?"

"Um, I'm not sure really. It'll be something." He conjectured as she continued to twirl loops of poesies around the outer corners of the page.

He dashed his fingers around the keyboard, always precise with an unconscious foreknowing, never clumsy. As he grew more confident in the groove of melody, he started to flick on the pre-set beats, tinkering like a chemist, unconcerned by its test tube ring – because he kept testing, until it sounded right.

"I like that one," Ava stopped briefly peering at him.

Damien nodded, furrowing his brow. "It's better if the pitch is lower, but this is as low as it can go." He flicked the pre-set beat off and just played the melody he had created unadulterated.

"It's like walking down the street, you know, when you see something you didn't expect." Ava stared up into the air of the room as her thoughts tumbled out of her mouth.

"I guess so," he figured.

"Not jumping out at you, but maybe just off to the side, something that was always there but you kept failing to notice." She put the end of the pencil in her mouth at her conclusion.

It was a cosseted charm created by the duality of creator and listener. Damien could be both, but with Ava there, she was endorsement. But an inner scepticism pummelled, relenting that its ultimate appeal would only be by the ears of those he could play it to – on the outside. Mrs White would be the litmus test. But the thought of playing it to her made him feel suddenly queasy. He had seen how she could play – complex pieces – sonatas, preludes and concertos of the highest order – classical music. What he wrote wasn't classical. It was something else. More like a jumble of everything he had been taught and everything he heard on the radio. John, he thought, was the only one who should be shown.

But it was Claudia who saw it first. She woke him splayed on the floor, half drooling onto his hand fast asleep late into the night, his pages scattered in front of him. She picked up the pages as he groggily stirred and marvelled at the minimalist Sanskrit harmony. Upon giving it a second look, was endeared at its borders, emblazoned with spaceships, stars and lightning rods that he had drawn. The one page was like an epigraph for the start of the rest of his life.

She placed the sheets back on the floor as she found them, encouraging him up and in to bed, hitting his head on the pillow with his gap-toothed hair. The upturned pages reflected the hand of its junior servant, some notes too eagerly written with a cursive stroke, others neatly erased and redrawn with a heavier lead. It was testament to an undertaking learned, an adaptation. With her dressing gown firmly wrapped around her, Claudia turned off the light as she departed the room, heartened by the lead of his pencil.

CHAPTER EIGHTEEN

Mrs White had started to give Damien cassette tapes with recordings of the pianoforte for him to play back. He had been given a tape deck for his last birthday gone. Herein lay Damien's ultimate mission to mars – the ability to record. He didn't have any blank tapes of his own, a conundrum that forced him to reap the best of what was already at hand. He placed the last tape Mrs White had given him into the deck and fast forwarded it until it neared its end and hit play. A twangy piano rang out into the room as though lost at the bottom of an empty jar until a clustered shuffle of buttons ended its hissing repertoire to a close, as though Mrs White had accidentally tripped over and clobbered her own tape deck to switch it off. The end of the tune meant a blank tape of bliss – it was open for him to fill.

He jammed the deck at the back of his desk closest to the wall in his room, so he could fit both his keyboard and sheet music in front of it. A final moment of procrastination dogged him. He wasn't sure where to start.

Cynthia had given him a tin of chocolates upon graduation of the fourth grade. At first discontent to touch them, he had very slowly picked at them until he had devoured them all. He had kept the tin. He opened it up and could still smell the scent of the chocolate once within it. He breathed it in, with its cocoa butter milk, still fragrant with a hint of strawberry and bitter candied orange. It smelt good. He closed the tin, its use was now predetermined. He housed it safely away in a box and put it back under his desk. He looked at the notes he had written and placed his hands on the keys. Now there was action. *Three, two, one...*record.

He delicately pressed down the keys feeling the pressure of their imagined pull-back and pound on internal strings, but this was more like thumping a water chestnut with a beat, it let out a subtle muted pound with each gentle press of his fingers.

He hit rewind.

From the clobbering shuffle close of the preceding piano, his came through with its electronic permeation. It sounded too light, like an old gramophone tincture. The keyboard lacked the piano hit of its hammers. He imagined it harder, punchier. That is what he'd hoped it would sound like to his ears in the room when he played it, but it sounded less so when he repeated it through mono. He needed something fuller. He had another idea. He took the tape recorder into the living room, pulling the coffee table close to the piano, where he placed the deck and posited himself on the stool. With his index and middle fingers he clicked down, then turned to the piano and played. He rewound and played the tape back.

"Hmpf," he sighed out a breath in frustration. It wasn't the way he wanted it. It sounded hollow, like an abandoned instrument drowning underwater. He sighed again as he stared up at the ceiling before sitting forward, resting his elbow on the edge of the piano, his chin on his hand. As he turned his head around in quiet vacillation, the home stereo at the other end of the room caught his eye. Frank had gradually been building it up over the years, from its humble radio and turntable components, to speakers and a tape deck. And there it lay in wait. It gave him an idea. Except Damien usually never touched it. It was off limits without permission. The problem expounded itself – he didn't want them to see or hear what he was doing. He wanted to do it quietly, alone. If it worked, then he would show them, surprise them with it.

Claudia wasn't home and Frank was out in the shed. He drummed the fingers of his right hand on the keys in front of him in a rapid-fire restlessness. What he wanted to do could only be done if he did it without asking, he thought. He winced as he knew he couldn't not ask.

"Grandpa," Damien approached Frank as he worked on an old generator in the shed down the back of the house, "would I be able to use the cassette player in the stereo?" He had asked it so forlornly thinking he had succumbed to giving up his freedom. Frank looked up at him quizzically, then beat back to Damien's surprise.

"Sure you can." He said.

Damien stared in a cross of perplexity and elation.

"Well, you are alright with putting it on aren't you?" Frank looked back down at the generator and turned the wrench around a nut in front of him, keen to keep his attention at hand.

"Yes, yes," Damien turned around in a half backwards gait back into the house.

Permission was granted. But if the living room was his soundstage, it was also a known thoroughfare - time was an essence in rapid evaporation. He raced into his bedroom and unplugged the keyboard from his desk and carried it into the living room and set it in front of the stereo before picking up the tape deck from the coffee table where he had last left it and placed it on the floor equidistant between the speakers of the stereo and the keyboard. He plucked out the tape from the deck and transferred it to the hi-fi stereo. He ran back into his bedroom and dug out an older tape from Mrs White and back in the deck fast forwarded it to a spot where it was clean. Now his symphony could begin.

He pressed record on the portable deck, then snapped down the play button on the stereo deck. His fingers soon followed landing upon the keys, playing in tandem the electric pulse of the keyboard with a backdrop of hammered piano strings that he buttered with a shimmering chime set beat. His eyes lit up at the sound as he grinned at a test that sounded more holistic and complete. Before he wound the tape back he felt a strange presence, something darker, a shadow lurking in the stillness of the room. Then he heard a soft scuffling behind him. He turned around and almost lost his breath.

Cynthia was standing in the doorway looking down at him on the floor in front of his keyboard. She had a gentle smile on her face equal parts grace and apprehension. Damien sat shocked staring up at her, not expecting to see her there. She was neatly dressed in a blouse and skirt and her hair was all done up. Rory coyly looked at him as he held Cynthia's hand, hiding behind his mother's skirt.

"Oh, hello." Damien blurted out aghast.

"Hello Damien, sorry I didn't mean to scare you." The air was silent. "That's interesting. What are you playing?"

Damien turned back around to the equipment. "Um, nothing really."

"Is grandma around?"

"No I don't think she is home yet." He half turned his head back to her.

"I'm going for a job interview. She said she would look after Rory. Did she tell you?"

Damien vaguely recollected Claudia having mentioned

something about his mother coming over, but had forgotten and hadn't really listened to what she had said. "Uh, I think so."

"Is grandpa here?"

"Yes, he's out the back." Damien looked up at her. Cynthia shuffled into the room and swung Rory into full view in front of him, kitted in denim overalls still a little too big, with a bowl haircut he was a bundle of cute, but shy in front of his older brother.

"Here, look after your brother for a few minutes." She let go of Rory's hand as she placed him on the floor where he sat beside Damien, waiting for the next cue anticipating it from his brother. Cynthia walked out of the room in search of her father leaving a trace of musk behind.

Damien swallowed the wince he wanted to make and turned to his brother making a frog face as Rory looked back at him doe eyed.

"Do you know what this is?" He said to Rory pointing at his keyboard. He nodded his head at him. "I can play you something." He played a few notes over the keys in front of his little brother. Rory continued to look at him with a curious innocence. "How about this." He played jingle bells, accompanying it with a bop of his shoulders. Rory giggled at him, which gave Damien the vigour to play him more, his reluctance quelled by the jubilation brought by his play. In the moments between melodies a car could be heard crunching up the driveway. Claudia was home. He could hear the muffled sound of conversation outside before hearing his mother's car leave.

He took advantage of having his brother there and asked to turn on the television. As Rory sat glued to Josie and the

Pussycats[7], Damien gathered his keyboard, sequestering it back into his bedroom, along with the tapes and deck which he still hadn't played back to hear its result. It was an undertaking for which he would have to reserve for later as he turned around and saw Rory had followed him into his bedroom like a kitten.

"Can I play with you?" he peeped out.

"Ah," he let out a long sigh. Rory's hands were devoid of anything. He had recalled he had always had some sort of toy in his hands any time he had gone out with them on the weekend. Now the only thing Rory carried was a look in his eye of desired inclusion with whatever it was Damien was doing. "Um." He ruminated in his head.

Matchbox cars, aeroplanes, a Tyrannosaurus Rex figurine and the pebble lined his windowsill. But they were Damien's treasured possessions and he didn't want his little brother's sticky fingers touching them. He pulled out his Rubik's Cube® from the box under his desk.

"You do it like this." He twisted it a few times in front of him illustrating the colour match before placing it in his hands. It would be enough to keep him tantalised for hours without him knowing exactly what he was meant to be doing with it. Rory twisted it a few times and looked up at Damien proving that point – that he had been handed a maze not solvable with its limited instruction and his primitive infancy. Damien took it off him.

He walked him back into the living room, where The Partridge Family was now showing, and placed him by the coffee table with some pieces of paper and coloured pencils. Rory drew as Damien sat watching the end of the show. A commercial appeared on the television for Frosted Flakes,

---

[7] Josie and the Pussycats is an American animated television series created by Dan DeCarlo and Richard Goldwater from Archie Comics. Hanna-Barbera Productions. 1970-1972.

with a bright smiling boy eating his cereal at the breakfast table, with his blonde hair and sunny disposition. He had to turn off the television by negative association. He felt a strange form of sick. Too many Pear Trees. Then Cynthia returned.

"Well, better get you home in time for tea." She took up Rory's hand walking him toward the front door. She turned to Damien before she headed out. "It's good to see you sweetheart." It was an effort. An effort she was trying to bring back to him. An effort he was trying to capture. Efforts were hard.

He watched as she packed Rory into the backseat of her car, a sight all too familiar, a sight to thwart all efforts. To watch was the torture of self-flagellation and an advertisement for everything wrong. Everything that must be wrong with him. *I'm not the blonde haired boy with the sunny disposition. Maybe then you would take me with you.*

Like a dispossessed mariner left on the shore, he watched the two red beady-eyed tail lights trail off down the drive.

*

A queasiness rose in his belly, like a boiling broth pulled from the heat that wouldn't settle. With the mix of overcooked insipid green peas and soggy cornmeal, he kept picturing the plate he had to part abandon and ask to be excused from the table to go to bed early. The mush he had half eaten squirmed in his stomach and permeated into his head making him dizzy. As he lay in bed, he rolled over and stared at the wall two feet in front of him. Its soft grey was visible from moonlight sneaking in through the window. He stretched out his hand and touched it. The wall was cool, its plaster on brick smooth like layers of paint covering sand. Close and contained. It made him know where he was, who he was. *I am here.*

He rolled over to the other side, where his eyes cast a line toward the window. The Tyrannosaurus Rex's cracked skin glimmered in the soft light. It made him think of a wasteland in which the beast had come. Maybe he could disappear to that wasteland, like the ones he had seen in the picture books, where there were no humans to cause him pain. If the moon had a dozen faces to light up like a candelabra it might have been enough to remove the gloom inhabiting him and everyone else to see in their self-imposed darkness. But that one face was enough for it to light up his tape deck tucked on his desk.

He rolled down the covers and crawled out of bed, hurriedly walking on the cold wood floor to pick up the portable player, absconding it back with him to his bed. His creation hadn't been played back yet and was lapping at the back door of his mind.

He rewound the tape back for a few seconds, then he hit play. Ava lay there on her belly on the other side resting on her elbows like a doe-eyed seal pup, and smiled at him in approval. Damien nodded back.

It sounded really good. It sounded even better in the dark.

CHAPTER NINETEEN

An Ordinary Time, where his brain felt like a sloth, dulled and loathsomely bored by the green of its cloth strapped altar, another monotonous scripture. Another speech he had heard what seemed like a thousand times before. They all sounded the same. It was the first time he had started to feel constricted, like a conscripted soldier who knew his number was up the moment it had been pulled from a canister, waiting in earnest for the diatribe of the war of words to end. *If Jesus was so wonderful, why wasn't he wonderful enough to take care of me?* Or was he confusing this with God – He was the one who looked down on you, but seemingly only if you were willing to be his servant, a servant who looked up. Fat lot of good he'd done for him. He didn't want to be a servant to anyone. The weekends that he wasn't asked to play music during proceedings were like being stuck in a train in a tunnel. Why Claudia and Frank made him come every Sunday when his mother did not was a procedure for which a session at the dentist seemed disappointingly infrequent by comparison and an unfair requirement.

For all the pain of obedience, Damien's patience was his victory, whereby the afternoon was all his. "Amen." He chided.

Damien and Patrick met up on their bikes at the central crossing and trailed their way down to the creek a mile north of the road, now that the snow had melted. They could hide under the pine trees sheltering out of view and conceal themselves, the rush of water muffling any correspondence, secrets left unexposed, surrounded by the scent of wet bark. Patrick coyly pulled out a cigarette from his shorts. They both guffawed in mischievous awe at its forbidden nature. Patrick had an older brother and had stolen the cigarette out of his brother's crumpled pack having beaten him out of bed one morning. The lighter would have been a red rag to a bull, so he had excluded it from his pilfering.

"Did you bring the matches?" Patrick probed.

"Yep." Damien soon followed pulling out the box.

"Here, light it," Patrick held it out in front of him.

Damien plucked out a match with his fingers and struck it down the side gingerly holding it aloft. Patrick moved the cigarette tip out under it. Patrick nonchalantly put the butt into his mouth while Damien examined the feat closely. "Here, you have one."

Damien picked it up like a fine specimen and did the same, placing it between his lips, more Brando than Dean. But neither pair were aware of the difference between the suck and the inhale and between the two of them tack-toed placing the cigarette in their mouths, naïve to the nature of breathing in.

"My brother holds them like this," Patrick mimicked a pose holding his thumb underneath and his index and middle finger on top, jutting out his chin as he placed the butt back in his mouth and pretend squinted the smoke from his eyes. "Girls hold it like this, so never hold it like this." He commandingly switched his fingers around to nestle the white paper tube between his fore and middle fingers in a V. Damien laughed at him stupidly. Patrick rolled his eyes, waving the cigarette in front of him. "You know a better way?"

Damien held it between his thumb and forefinger, "this is cool," he said. He had seen his father smoke before, but he seemed to do it less often when he was around, usually disappearing outside. That's where he caught the sight one night of the golden orange glow that ringed around the outer edge of the cigarette sticking out of his mouth, an ominous presence in the dark. He wondered how he could get that same fiery glow. He couldn't seem to do it. All he could see on the end was grey ash speckled black and white. Patrick stubbed it out with his foot when the end of the tether was reached, its evidence buried underground.

With the time abundant to eradicate the stench from their clothes, they straddled boulders at the creek slicing pebbles across the water, shattering its membrane into ripples.

"It's better with a slingshot." Damien declared.

"I don't have mine anymore."

"Where is it?"

"Ackerman stole it."

"He's a knuckle head."

"He's nobody."

"Nothing."

"Dusty."

"A knuckle duster." Damien felt the commanding power of his new-found branding of a class mate with a penchant for pinching and being as conceited as shit. "Should jump him one."

"Too right. But I'd like to see you do that." Patrick chastised.

"You don't think I can? I could if I wanted to." Damien postured back.

They sliced more pebbles, swinging their arms ripe for dislocation.

"That's why he's popular." Patrick contributed.

"Why?" Damien inflected up from his monotone.

"He's a charlatan." Patrick threw a rock that splashed and plopped.

"What's a charlatan?"

"A liar."

"Well he shouldn't be popular. He's a dick." He let out a huff of indifference.

"Slap stick dick." Patrick cut a fine slice which shimmied into a skid across the water flaying the water astride like the curling wings of a falcon where they both guffawed in admiration. "Ooh! Ha!"

"Aww! Brilliant!" Damien let his smile brim wide in the replicated astonished delight of his friend.

They curtailed their amusement in order to get back in time to each of their homes before nightfall's curfew. As Patrick swung his bike around waving him adieu, Damien reflected his friend's same gesture of goodbye. As he watched him trail off down the other end of the road in his own direction of home, it was like losing an arm, detached. A shudder of isolation had started to dog him whenever he watched Patrick depart. Anytime. Watching him get off the bus to walk toward his home, watching him ride off on his bike away from him, watching him walk up the long driveway to his house when Damien was on its precipice - watching him leave the scene of his line of sight. He hated it when he left him. It was a reminder of beady-eyed red tail lights he was forced to consume and the reconciliation of his surrender to a home without the things in it that should have always been there. The thing his friend had that he didn't. If Patrick had to ride one way, Damien had to ride the other. He rode to the only place he could.

As night fell into a space alone, it made way for a new

allure for which to attach himself - to watch Steve Austin dispel the myth that a man could not be remade into something better[8]. That's what he remembers they said at the start. He believed every word.

Like an arm detached he could put it back. A thing of disembodied parts could become whole again. Its metal would make him a machine. Unbreakable. Like Steve. But for all his bionic mettle, he still had a soul. You couldn't replace his soul. Though, in a frozen climate, not even a pumping heart could prevent him from breaking down. But that's all it was, a frozen heart that could melt and beat itself back in warmer climes. It was a notion that creeped in the gloom of an afternoon - he had to get out of this place. It was cold, wet, damp. The damp clung to his skin like a wet rag. Had he really been made of metal he'd rust. It was the cold that slowed. Maybe it was the cold that was breaking him.

He walked out the back door to prove his point. The hinge on the back screen door breathed out the breath of a thousand footsteps. In the night who knows where they led. He could see the fine drizzle of night-time rain. Through its splinters the leaves glistened like a shiny plastic, pounded by a scent of sodden soil. The place of trodden feet. He lost his train of thought at what he was trying to prove. He proved it was cold. Bitterly cold. That was all. He turned to walk back inside, but before reaching for the handle he noticed Ava leaning on the veranda rail to the side by the woodpile. She was looking out into the night away from him. The clematis dangled without its flower. He could see the mist of rain on her hair shimmer like crystal shards from the light of the window. She must have walked in from the rain. There was something pretty about the rain, he thought. He opened the door and stepped back into the warmth of the house.

---

[8] Steve Austin of the TV series *The Six Million Dollar Man* Opening dialogue from Population: Zero, *The Six Million Dollar Man* Season 1, Episode 1. Silverton Productions; Universal Television. 1974.

CHAPTER TWENTY

Stuck in a landscape that does not change, only with the seasons, was akin to being trapped in the same landscape in the picture frame adorning the wall of the living room that changed with the shadow casts of the sun, seasoned only with its hue. Damien felt trapped with the unchanging nature of the room, of its furniture, of the house, of the unchanging nature of silent afternoons.

He had been playing the piano for six years, advanced a year ahead and as he sat at its keys in the living room. Another run-through of a known sonata, minuet or allegro wasn't enough to evaporate the angst that thudded him late one day. He felt confused by it. An internal tremor ripped at him. He didn't know where it came from as he sat there not knowing what to do. He had been given instruction from the school conductor that they had wanted him to play solo Gershwin's

Summertime[9] for the school graduation assembly. Whether it was a swift manoeuvre of attention he sought or a mistaken acknowledgement of his prowess that he did not seek, it plummeted him into an anxiety he didn't know existed.

He had played to church congregations and in the school orchestra, but never alone. And of the plethora of eisteddfods and exams, the people were usually restricted to parents and other music students and their teachers. Here he was asked to play alone in front of a much bigger crowd. It was a change in the landscape. But one for which he was still alone in the picture frame. The view of that picture could be very alluring if he had wanted to be in it. Summertime appeared repulsively stifling.

He imagined all the faces that would be staring up at him. Some had seen him play before. He didn't know why it was bothering him now. He kept thinking of the baseball team pointing at him and calling him a loser. *Doesn't know how to throw a ball.* He had dropped the team and steered clear of watching them train and avoided Rick in the school halls as much to Rick's pleasure and Damien's disdain.

He had asked Mrs White if she had the sheet music, but it was a request to be emptied the moment he returned to school the following Monday. He went to see Mr Marshall, the school music teacher responsible.

"I can't do it," Damien nervously cut out of his mouth. "I'm sorry."

Mr Marshall stood tall and crossed his arms in front of him in a posture that looked as though he was about to scold him, for the days he had wasted when he could have given it to someone else. Damien nervously offered that option in

---

[9] Gershwin, George. "Summertime" from *Porgy and Bess*. 1935

advance.

"Someone else better than me should do it." He could feel his cheeks flush.

Mr Marshall stood unabated and furrowed his brow. He cocked his head, still eyeing Damien with a defiant accord Damien couldn't read, until he opened his mouth and unfolded his arms, clasping his hands in front of him.

"You are the one to do it," he said with commanding sympathy. "Take back your power Damien," he said to him resting his hand on his shoulder then moved away toward the classroom door, before opening it for him. "Come see me tomorrow at lunch time. You'll see you can do it."

Mr Marshall motioned the way out for Damien who swung his bag on his back and walked out the door. He didn't walk out with a skip in his step, possibly with more apprehension for a battle lost and a new front hastily advancing. But there was a confidence to Mr Marshall that deflected his fears and made him think that maybe everything would be ok. Maybe it was possible.

The panic of his new duty plunged and dipped. That afternoon he walked over to Mrs White's house straight after school rather than going home. He had already wasted days and didn't want to wait until tomorrow. Playing in front of Mr Marshall suddenly loaded him with dread.

He walked up the path past her picket fence and tapped on her front door, until her face appeared through the screen.

"Oh, hello Damien. Today's not the usual day for you is it?" She pushed the screen door open. He hung on her welcome mat.

"Um, have you got Summertime, the sheet music?" His nerves bit. He didn't know why. He knew her well. The song he didn't.

"Come on in."

She fumbled through some baskets of booklets and shelves stacked with manuscript in her piano room.

"I'm sure I have that one somewhere." She stuck her finger to the bottom of her lip. Damien looked on more frantic than her search, wishing she would speed it up. "Oh I know." She reached into a cupboard and pulled out a book. "It's a new one."

Damien suddenly relaxed, then impulsively shot out of his mouth. "Can I try and play it now?" A knee jerk that made her suddenly dither on the spot. He immediately stood assured in front of her, a person he knew well enough to ask properly. "Would you be able to teach me the first few bars?"

She was charmed by his presence and happy to relent to his request. He hadn't even told her what it was for yet. She sat by the piano and bade him to take a seat. The shame of wanting to give in died and made way for the eagerness to have the people he hoped would be there to see him play.

CHAPTER TWENTY-ONE

Summer burned with a brightness supplanted by the echo of four hundred hands clapping. So much so he was happy to stay inside in his room throughout the holidays and dream on repeat the approbation to which he now committed to memory. The musical fugue of admiration trickled through his brain and it was where he learned he could be adored. The hours he had practised were the credits rolling at the end of the film. His teachers brimming from the wings, the advocacy running the reel.

If he could duplicate himself and run in a contrapuntal motion, one row was heaven and the other hell. He now knew upon which tracks he wanted to chase. The empty room in which he found himself was itself a false entry in a life that didn't have to be his. There was only one way to rid it of its emptiness.

He pulled out his turntable and placed on some singles, one after the other. With a fresh sheet of paper in front of him, he started to transcribe the notes he heard from the songs playing. He repeated their run until he had distilled them down to their very last note, his comprehension of them tested when he played back over the keyboard what he had scribed. These weren't the classical pieces he had been taught to play, nor the simple boyish compositions he had made up himself. They were the music he wanted to play. He knew he could replicate something similar for himself. It was the first time he tried.

It was a glimmer.

"Let me hear you play," John had requested one day. It wasn't a request for an exposition of the tutored, but a request for a display of the newly created. John had learnt of what had been occupying Damien for the entirety of the holidays. But Damien had either been too shy or too protective to show anyone what he was making. John was the first to give it a prod after he stopped in one day to see how Damien was.

"What would you like to hear?" Damien asked as John sat with him in his bedroom.

"Have you written anything for yourself?"

Damien sniffed out the direction in which he was going. "You mean like a song of my own."

"Yeah." John carefully hid his keen.

"Um, I wrote a short piece. It's just a chorus." Damien warned as an admission of the newly inaugurated.

Damien consulted the keyboard. He flicked on a beat that set a rhythm to complement the eight bar refrain, a bright pulse for his fingers to follow. His fingers struck the keys. He replayed it four times through, its rondo creating a length resembling a song. It was devoid of the infancy of his previous tinkering, sounding more like a piece due for adult ears. Worthy of this man before him to be the first to listen.

John let out a breath, impressed.

Before allowing a smile to spread from ear to ear, Damien searched out John's face to perceive the genuineness of the claim to which he professed.

"Well, it's a start. I'm still learning." Damien quickly submitted, then leaned back into the chair, nerves faded by a will to relax.

There was an aura of the future. As they sat there together Damien's posture was a signal for the potential in life, a stance through early practise and the bearing of anticipation. It was an image too premature for Damien to yet understand the intoxicating undertaking in which he was about to submit. To commence writing music – he didn't know what he was doing, yet he did. His experience and initiated attempts scratched on the surface like a cat at the back door. The force of its zeal determined whether you opened it to find a predator or a kitten. Damien knew he was going for it full force.

To play in front of this man gave him the confidence that it was something he could do, that someone was interested. Even if it was just the one, it was one more than it was before. He fumbled in his brain what it might be like to play something he had written in front of his peers, wondering if they would deliver the same applause as what they had before. Their commendation had been a surprise and had left him excited by what he could do. But it too brought a reminder of the nerves he had experienced before he ascended the stage. The stage reminded him of the faces of kids in his class. The class reminded him of the painful moments sitting in the middle of the room, when everyone was chatting except for him, or walking down the corridors hoping to be acknowledged when no-one said anything to him at all – because he knew he was inferior. The school assembly had brought more stares. People started to look at him more, some smiled in passing. He didn't know if it was because they had admired what he had done or if it merely had placed him in a spotlight, as though he had grown a few inches taller and he now met their line of sight. Whatever the reason, he had to put the nerves behind him. Their commendation on that day made him feel better.

He closed the page ablaze with his cursive stroke and squirrelled away the book into a drawer in his desk. He followed John out to the car to wave him goodbye. Back in his room he looked at the music books that sat stacked alongside text books. He hoped they were all impressed by his effort. *He* knew what effort was. He hoped they noticed it all. Maybe it was a sign it was time to *show* them, as telling hadn't helped him at all.

CHAPTER TWENTY-TWO

A disco ball beamed out cherry, apricot and butter lights, falling in a twisted candy cascade upon the youth under its bulb. They twirled in solidarity with the leaves on the trees outside that lit up their Jeffersred in the same shade in the dark when hit by headlights. Parents dropped their children off at the hall in the centre of town.

Damien housed a soda in a plastic cup as he tentatively waited at the side of the hall for Patrick to show up. He sipped it intermittently as he fretfully watched the double doors praying for his friend to make a hurried entrance. Some eager parent had already adorned the frame with a wreath, some sixty days before Christmas was due. On second thought, it may have been left from the Christmas before, forgotten. He turned his attention to the floor.

Damien flicked furtive glances at the pre-pubescent girls

as they held hands jigging to You Should Be Dancing[10]. It was a pity Damien wasn't because he liked the song - he'd heard it on the radio. Their glossy smiles and pony tails sheening under the lights and the ease with which they moved themselves was truly mesmerising - and frightening. Here in this room with glittering lights, they made him want to run into the middle of the room and bathe under them, but were somehow refracted by the angels dancing underneath, making him want to run in the opposite direction in terror before they could see him watching them. He was afraid they may potentially drag him in to join them. It was a notion he coveted yet felt equally repulsed by sure it might be the death of him. They looked like they were having so much fun. Girls were depressing. *Patrick, where are you?* He felt his stomach do backflips. He looked down at his watch, trying to glimpse its hands in the flashes of light. By the time he looked up he had emerged.

So there stood two awkward boys with their soda cups watching from the sideline. The song had changed and the lights pummelled out blue green. It signalled a change from shocking to subdued, making him more aware of the solitary stance he had chosen and the glue of apprehension wedging his feet, too frightened to submerge himself where he had never been. After so many refills and sips of his soda, he had to relieve himself, the perfect intermission away from the scene. But by the time he returned he didn't want to stay poised in the same position. He started to walk around the hall.

One of the mothers from another of his friends in his class, who had come as a chaperone, recognized him as he loitered around the drinks table on its third pass.

---

[10] Gibb, Barry & Gibb, Robin & Gibb, Maurice. "You Should Be Dancing" from the album *Children of the World*. Performed by The Bee Gees. RSO. 1976.

"Is that you Damien?" She asked.

He recognised her in the semi dark. "Hi Mrs Phillips."

"You having fun?" She beamed a smile at him as she bopped her hips that made the wing swept fringes of her hair bounce in unison. "Get out there in the middle. Mark is there, see, take a look." She pointed her finger to the middle of the dance floor.

Damien nodded in acknowledgement seeing his classmate jigging within the swarm.

"Go on, go out there." She encouragingly pressed, until it became apparent she wasn't going to have her instruction taken for granted and gave him a second nudging look.

Damien walked towards the middle of the floor, just to get away from the humiliation of her detection of the unsureness for which he felt. There in the middle he squirreled himself in, where he found some faces he knew and to his surprise Patrick who had managed to shunt himself into the cluster without him knowing where he had disappeared to.

The songs churned over and the lights teased his eyes until he closed them and just let himself sway with the sound of the music. He lathered in its bursts. It was the thump of the beat with its vibrations through the floor that was the ultimate elixir creating a propulsion within his body to stomp as though his legs were fists needing to punch. Here lay a new release that he could physically enact removed from the tendrils of imagination. He shuddered and shunted his body in time to the music and beat out his breast that cracked open the hunch of his shoulders and rid the tension consuming him until he forgot where he was.

When he opened his eyes, there was a girl from his grade staring at him. She gave a sweet smile when his eyes met hers as she quickly shuffled away with her girlfriends. Her name was Elyse.

The lights tangled like a creeping vine that made him slow his pace and stand in a gentle sway to gain a centred place. His peers jostled around him until he stood still. He could feel his heart flutter. He gave Patrick a gentle tap and pointed his finger signalling his exit. He nervously skirted the perimeter of the dance floor as he had before, this time with a coy glance trying to see where she went. He couldn't see her or her friends and headed toward the main doors.

The heat of the room inhabiting his body expelled itself as a foggy mist of breath as he walked outside. The biting midnight cold of autumn had descended early. A stream of parked cars were waiting out front. He watched as a couple of kids scooted into the back seat of one and depart. He looked around inconspicuously and couldn't see her anywhere. Maybe she had left. He walked around the side of the hall, where he stumbled upon an older boy pressed against a teen girl from an upper grade along the side wall kissing. The flutter in his heart fell into a squirminess and he ducked back quickly in the direction from which he had come.

Standing out the front looking back toward the open doors into the hall was like looking into a kaleidoscope flanked by blackness. He didn't know whether to go back inside. Maybe she was still in there. He looked at his watch. Mrs Arncliffe was going to be picking them both up in half an hour's time.

He trailed his way back in and found a line back to his friend, who was casually pouncing around with the bounce of the beat. Damien cut through the crowded space and took up another soda from the sidelines. He found a quiet spot and rested his back against the wall, more outfield than midfield. He remembered the conversation he had had with Patrick's father that day – maybe this was how you could catch someone with your eyes, off to the side – not to catch out, but to catch the beauty of those eyes upon him and the flutter in which they beat within him. You could notice things better to the side. He drank up the movement of the room in front of him. They were as good as the bubbles within the soda in his cup. The fact he couldn't actually see her anywhere made him relax.

Within the throng shy hands held, bad dance timing revealed itself, happy faces remained regardless. At the side, the centre was where he wasn't and shunted him with a reminder – he was different from the mesh in front of him making him reluctant to go back in to join them. Nervousness spiked his drink. He left the soda on a nearby table and idled back around the outskirts of the dancing circus so he at least didn't look like he was doing nothing at all. But the circle had enclosed rather than opened, shunning the boy on the outside of it.

He dawdled at its perimeter, then relented to head back outside. He sat on the step at the foot of the hall. He looked at his watch. It would be over soon.

CHAPTER TWENTY-THREE

Elyse hadn't come to class today. She had been wearing the same festive red and green pullover nearly every day somehow forgetting its celebration was long over. It was a small detail he had noticed after watching and looking out for her for months, ever since that night she had stared at him under tumbling lights.

He hadn't paid much attention to her before. He saw she was number six on the class chart for the last mathematics test, five places below him. It gave him a level of pride in knowing the girl in sixth place. Except he didn't really know her at all. Although he had started to take account of her friends. Her friend Carly sat there the same way Elyse did, diligently paying attention, in a bright lemon t-shirt with her jeans flaring under the desk, visible today thanks to the vacancy of the seat next to her. Despite the sunniness of her attire, Carly wasn't who he was thinking of. He was wondering where Elyse was, hoping she would be back tomorrow. He pondered what she might wear, maybe something new, more like the flowers of spring.

Carly and Elyse were in the equestrian club and he had seen them mount their horses in a paddock once when Frank drove past in the truck one weekend. He remembers her graceful spine, the way she rose as though aided by a delicate ribbon. He noticed the horse was a gelding. He had seen a horse castrated before, strapped by the ankles until it fell with its bulbous mass strangled with a string. He wondered if she knew of the corruption that had occurred underneath her seat.

He reacquainted his attention to the book in front of him, with only twenty minutes left to read through the rest of the agriculture text before the next bell. The final chapters were about the different species of bats and the conundrum of their being beneficial in killing insects and birds that threaten crops yet pose a threat to livestock and orchards. The pest and the pollinator and disperser of seed who could build a tree for the bird that it killed. It seemed an incongruous creature.

Frank was friends with a farmer who owned livestock. Damien had been down to their property one weekend when he was younger and when he had walked into the shed there was a rifle mounted on the wall. "For shooting the bats," his grandfather's friend had said. At the time he didn't know what he was referring to – bats were in comics. His reference was to the ones in the air, he had realised, after they had gotten back in the truck to go home on the cusp of dusk and Frank had pointed out the winged creatures flying through the semi dark sky.

He wondered how effective that was to shoot them with a gun, where they flew so high and depending where you looked resembled a hundred vampire winged poppy seeds spinning through the air. How did you know what you were shooting?

A mammal that could fly. But it wasn't a bird. It didn't have a beak, with a hidden tongue. He laughed to himself. They too had a tongue, but instead they had teeth. A warm-blooded animal that liked to feed on the blood of other animals from a group of species that also liked to feed on nectar. Did that mean blood tasted sweet? He stared at the picture of a giant golden-crowned flying fox hanging upside down, wrapping his leather-like shawl around him. He looked positively regal. No wonder - he knew he could build habitats. But his distant brother the vampire was the ugliest with a face like a minced-up bulldog, whose nectar was blood. He didn't scatter seeds or pollinate flowers. How could anything grow from ripping the neck of another animal?

He looked up at the empty desk two rows ahead. It made him think of the tube-lipped nectar bat who injected its long tongue into the depths of a flower. Incongruous. She was made of flesh and blood.

The bell rang and he closed his book.

The backs of the heads of all the children sitting in front of him on the school bus on the way home summoned his stare. Just from the backs of their heads he knew who they were instantly, knew where they lived, could place them with their whole families in a picture frame along with their white picket fences and the church pew they addictively coveted like the best seats in the cinema house. Some were not as clear to decipher through the growth of their childhoods. To pass the time he played the game of guess. He gave himself a point for every correct estimation and a subtraction for every wrong one as they disembarked this flight ship to heaven or hell. He was up three points by the time he got off the bus, that was after he added back one of the minuses after he could not accept he got Davy wrong, his neighbour, all because his mother had given him the most unfortunate of home haircuts making the back of his head look like a rat with a mite infection. He was instantly relieved there was one thing he did not receive from his mother – a home haircut. At least Claudia had the tenacity to send him in to the local barber.

He bounced a tennis ball all the way up the stretch of road after the bus dropped him off, passed the stumps of Elms replaced with Cottonwoods. Each time he pumped it up and down he had a strange desire for something not there. Not that it was explicit. It was just a sensation, like a nerve, not pinched but subtly stroked. He didn't know what that *something* was either. The road in front of him was blank territory too many times trodden that lead to the same driveway. There were only so many times he felt he could walk it. But then again there were only so many months left until the school year was through and a new take on life in the upper grades was to begin. He was looking forward to something new. Like a haircut. Fresh. Then he received an invitation, unexpectedly.

CHAPTER TWENTY-FOUR

It was Spring break. Frank and Claudia had driven interstate to attend an agricultural show. Cynthia had asked Damien home to stay for the whole holidays, an offer he both couldn't reject and was curiously happy to accept. It was a gold nugget. She had asked for the week off work, but the time was of his choosing to do whatever he wanted. The house was within walking distance to the town's central shopping strip where there were arcade games. That in itself was enough of an enticement for Damien to think his stay could be worth its weight in gold.

"Be good for your mother," Claudia nudged as she departed.

Cynthia had been working at a local business and had saved up the money to buy him a new top-of-the-range fold out bed. She pulled it out setting it up in the middle of his brother's room. The sheets smelt of fresh soap powder, a soft starchy white, laid out as crisp as napkins carefully folded upon a table at a dinner party. As he lay in the bed the first night, he looked around, observing all the things that inhabited his brother's bedroom. He counted the things on the shelves. There was the odd figurine, a bear and a couple of other toys. His brother didn't have as many things as he did. But his brother's life was only just beginning. Damien felt like his was already half way through. The spines of picture books jutted out upon the dresser. He remembered his mother reading one of them to him. That was a long time ago.

She had lined up packets of Cocoa Puffs®, Frosted Flakes and Sugar Smacks® on the breakfast table the first morning.

"I wasn't sure which one you would like," she said. He was staggered by the display. He wasn't usually allowed to have them at home. But equally stunned as to the demeanour with which she had offered them, a mix of asking for endorsement and permission. He decided to accept them.

"Cocoa Puffs, thanks."

Cynthia sat in front of him with buttered toast and a black coffee. She started to open the packet of Sugar Smacks for Rory, until his brother pointed to the Cocoa Puffs saying he wanted the same as Damien. Rory's acceptance of them was far from understated, becoming obvious such a treat was not bestowed regularly and he understood why he had beamed such a huge smile at Damien when he had entered the room to sit down. He had been chafing at the bit waiting for Damien to join them as Cynthia asserted they couldn't start until Damien arrived at the table.

The linoleum squeaked of cleanliness underfoot. The kitchen bench was neatly stacked with a row of shiny white enamel canisters, a coffee maker and toaster, its laminate clear of anything else, not even a single crumb spotted it. She had cleaned.

"How did you find last term?" She inquired.

"It was ok." He scooped up a spoonful of Cocoa Puffs and sunk them into his mouth.

"Getting harder?" She nudged in interest.

"Mm, I can do it." He shrugged his shoulders

nonchalantly as the puffs popped in his mouth of milk.

"I thought maybe if you are interested we could go and see a movie?" She proffered gently sipping from her coffee mug, moving to change the subject.

"Ah yes," Damien nodded casually.

"Is there anything you would like to see?"

The question was a slightly futile one for the limited offering available to them at the Citadel Cinema – which was just a theatre room at the town hall. If a reel hadn't caught up to them yet or had already been shipped on you had to drive over an hour and half into the city to see what they had that you didn't. He didn't think his mother would be in a mood for a long drive. He had already seen the one that was currently playing, but he was never against a repeat viewing, if not for the popcorn and soda.

"Anything is fine."

She took them both out for burgers afterwards. The shop next door to the burger bar had a pinball machine and some arcade games. Tank[11] and Death Race[12] was all that was on Damien's mind all day.

"Can I have some money for next door?" He asked his mother for some change. She gave him a couple of coins.

"Don't be too long." She quietly instructed, then Rory looked at the exchange soliciting a suggestion to be able to join him just by the pleading look on his face. "Take your brother." She gently suggested, pulling out her purse to give him another coin.

Damien wanted to roll his eyes, but did what he was told. As he followed him into the arcade, it was company that

---

[11] Tank is an arcade game developed by Kee Games of Atari, Inc. 1974. Designed by Steve Bristow and Lyle Rains.

[12] Death Race is an arcade game by Exidy. 1976.

wasn't in breach of his desired solitude as Rory happily stood by him watching how he played the games. Damien became unconsciously happy he was there in a show of his adeptness.

"You nearly got that one." Rory exalted with excitement of the hits and misses on the screen.

"Yeah, nearly." Damien answered on auto pilot.

Rory shot up a glimpse at his brother in an effort to read what the best thing to say to him was. He quietly looked on at the screen as Damien pounded away at the controls. As he ran out of coins, he allowed him to step to the front and have a go. Rory's height restricted the better angle that his brother's years gained, but nevertheless perched upon his toes and bashed at the buttons and knobs on the console until the screen read "Game Over".

Cynthia sat silently flicking through a magazine waiting for them at the once occupied table until the two human beings she had made strolled back into view. Rory was a miniature version of the boy she once knew, somewhere locked in her memory. He had grown passed the halfway point of Damien who was on the verge of sprouting out of being a boy.

"Was that good?" She piped up with a smile to both of them, badly hiding a repression of sadness.

"Yeah," Rory beamed back. Damien couldn't help but crack a smile too.

Out in the street as they headed to the kerb to cross the road, Cynthia automatically held out her hand searching for Rory's before crossing, calling gently "hold my hand." She immediately turned her head to Damien in a repeated gesture of safety. Their eyes met and recoiled as awkwardly and quickly as her hand. He was old enough to hold his own in crossing the road. Time had missed its progress.

She was wearing flared jeans. All he could remember was

their swishing sound as they walked to the other side back to the house. He'd walked beside her down the street, up the street, across the road, to the car, from the car, into her house, out of her house so many times before, he didn't know why this was the one time he noticed the sound of her. A sound through friction.

He brought his tape recorder and played tapes for Rory, where his brother bopped around the room in front of him, carrying the unaffectedness of his age. They played Monopoly® and he taught him how to play UNO®. They watched television in the evening. Anything he wanted. The living room, with its shag carpet that was in wild contradiction to the delicate lace curtains that hung across a large bay window, whose hue changed from bright honeysuckle with the morning's eastern sun through to amber with the evening's lamplight, was a place wrought. Bent into a shape that was as twisted as the world he thought he was inhabiting. It was so neat and perfect.

But this place was not his place and all the accoutrements of his home were beginning to become sorely missed the longer the week went on. He missed Claudia and Frank. It was a strange combination of emotions to miss what he desperately wanted to get away from in order to run to here. As soon as he was ready to go home, he felt a sudden surge that he was running out of time to lap up the last of what was there, except there were no crumbs on the floor to lick up, he had already scoured up all he could find.

"Now that I have the bed, you can come over more often if you want to." She urged with fretful recompense.

"Oh, ok." He shrugged a shoulder at her.

"Better than the sleeping bag on the lounge." She let out a nervous laugh, an attempt to persuade him with pointless candour.

But it was an offer all too late in the coming and one he

didn't think he particularly wanted. The bed, like its gesture, could be pulled out when it suited her, or when he otherwise had no choice, seeming more like an object of something to prove. It was an offering for which he wouldn't succumb, for its impermanence. A reminder he was always a visitor.

The bed had lost its meaning the moment he had to pack his suitcase and leave this Hotel California[13] to go back home. He bit the nugget and it broke his tooth. Leaving home to go home. It didn't make any sense. Cynthia was trying to patch and mend something that was torn. Torn by circumstance. But stitches always left marks in their fabric. The thread was a cord being forever tugged, something to heal that was painful to look at, a push pull from which he could never retreat. If only the cord was like the taper in a Christmas cracker, that you could pull until it cracked, snapped free from the opposite pole. Where something good may exist in one of the ends. But there were never any pieces of gold inside those crackers. Only bits of plastic. Or a fortune cookie if you had spent the extra dollars for the more expensive ones. Not that he was going to find his good fortune on the scrap of paper in a cracked cookie. He was too smart for that. He would make his own fortune.

And for all the substance of a Confucian Ode he started to disbelieve the things people told him. Pre-rehearsed lines cut into scraps and tucked into crevices hoping he'd find them, understanding what they meant. With them came an interpretation open for him to ignore, at least that was what he was now telling himself.

To be there with her those holidays was a stilted reality that was never really going to be his. One for which made him happy to be going back to his own bed. But nonetheless

---

[13] Felder, Don & Henley, Don & Frey, Glenn. "Hotel California" from the album *Hotel California*. Performed by The Eagles. Asylum. 1977.

leaving him with an anxiety over *what if I never return*. It made him feel sad, which only fed a hatred at the thought of wanting to stay. It made him feel sick that he ever thought it. He couldn't wait to get back home so he could stop the slide.

"I didn't think you liked it there anyway," Ava caressed.

It was a statement-cum-rhetorical question for which he did not want to provide a degree of subservience by honouring her with a response. Did he like it or not? He bit his tongue. He wanted to keep it to himself.

"It doesn't matter, you're home now," she completed what she started, now all too familiar with the silent stretches of Damien's taciturn responses – responses of deflected stares so she could read nothing at all. Regardless, her senses sapped up everything exuding out his pores, a sweat of dismay.

It just left him with a feeling of wanting to rip at something, anything, a tear so shrill in its severing of fabric you'd feel the pain of its noise in your spine as your eyes witnessed the splinters, rip at "it doesn't matter", because it did. It mattered too much. Everything that mattered he just spun around and around in a weave of folded up canvas, hiding everything on the inside.

CHAPTER TWENTY-FIVE

Chlorophyll. If this is what the foci of his biology classes were going to entail in the upper grades he wasn't sure for how long he could endure them. He had pre-read such details in the encyclopaedia at home years before. He thought he had heard rumblings about dissecting frogs. That would have been far more palatable. Until the teacher mentioned something about absinthe. It distracted him.

Chemical formulas dotted the paragraph making him think he should be paying attention and returned his focus to the page and his teacher.

"Chlorophyll absorbs energy from the sun."

Two stages being a reaction then a cycle - one in the light, the other in the dark - to synthesise itself into existence. He started to drift. *Absinthe*. He had heard the word before and tried to think from where. It was stuck somewhere in his memory. He became lost in thought.

Patrick distracted him by covertly slipping a trading card underneath his text book on the desk. Patrick and Damien had been swapping trading cards during lunch breaks. Damien had more to spare because other than his grandmother, Cynthia had been asking for them when she bought groceries, solicitously passing them on to Claudia every odd week on the quiet. He collected his new form currency trading them for just about anything. But another trading card wasn't what he needed. Patrick had a poster that Damien wanted. It was something that Damien did not have. Despite his attempts at securing it, it was something he was yet to attain. He turned to Patrick and tried to sneak the card back to him with a Morse coded shake of the head. His teacher sniffed out the exchange down the aisle.

"Boys, save it for after school." He sharply quipped staring in their direction. The end of the day was hours away, the prospect of the wait through a session in which he couldn't concentrate was equivalent to death in the afternoon[14].

He stared out the window. He could make out the A-frames of pine trees in the distance. He wondered if he could measure how far away they were. If he walked out of the room and traced a path counting his footsteps along the way and covered them as he went, would anyone have noticed that he had disappeared someplace else, not knowing where he went? Treading past the line of measurement led a deeper path where creatures surround and prowl. The moment he stepped on a thistle it became too painful and he had to turn back.

A cloudiness inhabited the room. He drew his attention back to its subject. The merging of light into dark and that something small could survive through it, the dark bit, momentarily fascinated him. A phasing then passing out the other side, but not as an object or a plant stuck, rooted in one place waiting for an external force to complete its orbit, but as a form of matter, a vapour transforming into something else.

---

[14] Hemingway, Ernest. *Death In The Afternoon* 1932. First Edition. Vintage Classics, Random House UK. 2000. It is both a non-fiction book about bullfighting as well as a cocktail the author invented which is made of absinthe and champagne.

That was the sugar. He drifted again. There was no sweetness in the air he breathed. The teacher's voice irritated and a squeak of the chair leg against the floor in front of him shrilled like a nail in the base of his spine that spread into every nerve. The air became sour.

A pressure was suddenly felt in the front of his head. He looked ahead trying to refocus, to conform to the container in which he was in. But he wanted to break the container. Its shape was stifling him creating a compulsive urge to punch it. The room started to spin and he felt his head become light.

Patrick looked to the side and noticed something queer in Damien's face. He wasn't sure if he was nodding off or on the verge of a seizure. He flicked at his heel under the desk. The explosion so intense within him suffocated his chest until it jolted him to.

Absinthe. He couldn't remember. He knew it, but he couldn't remember why.

CHAPTER TWENTY-SIX

Explosions came in two forms. One of them gave him the headiness of a wet dream. He looked down at himself under the sheets. A skinny freak of nature or something as weird as how he felt lay underneath. A body trying to catch up. Separating body from the feelings that now came with it was the only way to reconcile the two. Depending on what he thought of, their synthesis was combustible.

Both forms of explosion brought a shame as soiled as the stained pants buried deep into the bottom of the bed. Yet both brought a euphoria. Enough to exalt him out of bed and slap on his clothes for the day ahead.

He had been selected as an introductory youth nominee to play the local youth band, an accompaniment to girls that twirled their batons (as well as themselves) pre and mid ball game, less like a cherry, more like a garish topiary garnish. He was initially excited for the opportunity and at first it fulfilled his aspiration to be part of it. It was a big deal. But before too long it took a different tone - when he learnt where he stood. Mostly in the outfield. That along with physical education classes were equivalent to a stoning. Mingling among and standing in front of his brotherhood was enough to transform his shoulders into a sad wisteria's, hunched. They spoke with such bravado in the locker room, where they started to measure their manhood. There was something about the way they held themselves. They were a put down without even needing any words to be said.

The thumping from the stands droned through his skull with the force of a jet engine. It was the only consolation for being there, it was mesmerizing and made him zone out. A song vibrated itself into his mind.

We Will Rock You[15]. The song drilled through his head. Memorized.

But he wasn't a boy anymore. He was changing. Phasing.

Freddie. Now there was a man, Damien thought. He exuded a masculinity that dripped with a sensuality Damien was yet to comprehend. Tight pants and leather jackets. A sexuality that didn't matter what way he went. All that mattered was how it made him feel. The feeling gave him power. The thudding, the thumping, bashing, pumping. The sound of clapping. It brought him back to where he wanted to be. Where he knew the euphoria. God it felt good. And he knew the men who owned the stage. Made it theirs. He wanted to be just like them. He could be like them. He could be confident like them. He could own it.

Owning it owed control. A euphoria he could control. When he played music he learnt he could take it where he wanted it to go - to potent heights, whether through the volume of his radio or through the hard press of his fingers. Then there it comes...the applause. He knew it, he'd felt it.

He wondered what happened when the sound of clapping stopped, or worse if there was none at all. The sound of one

---

[15] May, Brian. Song "We Will Rock You". From album *News of The World*. Performed by Queen. EMI UK. 1977.

hand clapping[16] is a wave off the stage. *Did that mean they don't like you? How do you make them like you?* He thought, as he sat in the stand, his thoughts muffling the cheers around him, the whistle and gallop of feet on turf. It was a moment of stillness.

Then Rodney dropped his symbol with a resounding clang. "Oops, sorry," he peeped as he clumsily picked it up.

It was a not so subtle persuasion back into the land of reality and the green field held in his vision in front of him. There was only half an hour left of the game until Frank came around to collect him. He was sitting over the other side of the stand where he could also see Ben. Cynthia and Rory sat on the other side of them waving some streamers the colours of the home team. He could see them from where he sat. Good feelings plunged back into his being. For a moment he wondered what they were thinking about. It didn't really matter. They were all there.

The band weaved its way out like a centipede decorated with brass and sticks and drums. Damien commanded his assault on the skin of the drum. Its reverberation could be felt through the stick providing reassurance of the authority in which he had directed it. They wove their way in a loop to the other side. As they played their last tune, a girl was spun, batons were thrown, the players left, the crowd cheered. Damien's head was to the back of Frank, his mother and brother. The sounds around him petered out like a concertina file relaxing itself.

"Still going to get you on the tuba," Frank light heartedly nudged Damien on the arm as they met up at the entrance gate.

Damien smiled back and rolled his eyes in response.

John held out his hand in which Damien motioned

---

[16] Zen koan

forward to shake as he playfully pulled his hand away poking his finger into Damien's abdomen.

"Hey!" Damien squirmed backward, the childishness of the youthful boy hadn't yet escaped him or his mother's friend. Cynthia moved toward him as though she wanted to reach her hand out to stroke his head but stopped herself.

Despite the enthusiasms of this audience, he had a nonchalance at returning to the field behind him. It was down to another band he was keener to pursue. Though, in either band he didn't want to be its junior accessory. And the drums weren't what he wanted to play.

John walked beside him as they made their way to the car park.

He loaded himself into the truck and wound the window down, waving his mother and Rory goodbye, each going their separate ways, as Frank started the engine and eased forward trailing the way out the dirt driveway. He watched as John swung his keys around from his fingers clasping them in the palm of his hand and turned to walk toward his car, his plaid shirt tucked into jeans with cowboy boots, a familiarity that was part of the father he remembered. It seemed in stark contradiction to the whites of Damien's attire.

The truck was quiet during the drive on the way home. It had the scent of contained mustiness from its antique interior and as the truck shimmied over bitumen cracks and grooves, its squeaking clink was more audible in the silence. It's motion was comfortable.

He twirled the white cap he had worn in front of him in his hands. It characterized a generation he wasn't sure belonged to him. An attire that wasn't the one he wanted to wear. It was a prescription to a certain conformity. Though, its dictation wasn't something to which he had to adhere - he was old enough now - he could choose. He would have to mould himself to fit in with it or remould himself into something else. Something was going to fit him, he knew it had to be out there to fit, he pondered, as he stared at the wide but equidistant street lights counting them as the truck drove on.

CHAPTER TWENTY-SEVEN

It was raining outside. He could hear I Dream of Jeannie[17] leaking in from the living room where Claudia had it playing on the television. The day after New Year's Eve – its tone was as bleak as the afternoon on the other side of his window. He'd spent the previous two nights at Patrick's, tucked into a sleeping bag on the sofa, where they had watched Midnight Special[18] for its last show of the year.

Being here back in his room he plummeted. He'd lost his wings for flight, like a bat that doesn't fly in the rain. Or a bird with sodden wings. Whether it was Jeanie's jingle dripping into his room or the rain falling from the sky as it spattered like angry knuckles upon the slate roof, they interfered with the outlook. It was too cold, a frozen sort of cold. The cold rebound off his walls confining him, spreading fast from the flame red effects of the cold on his fingers making him close to numb. He opened his mouth and made mist pops of vapour into the icy air that disintegrated like

---

[17] *I Dream of Jeanie* is a TV sitcom. Sidney Sheldon Productions & Screen Gems & Sony Pictures Television. 1965-1970.

[18] *The Midnight Special* is a TV Music Show. Burt Sugarman Productions. NBC Studios. 1972-1981.

 bursts of white bubble gum. If only they tasted as sweet. Maybe his breath was closer to the mushroom clouds of an atomic bomb. It was hot. It made sense.

Patrick had turned the television up loud as they watched the music show the night before last. They ate Cheetos® and popped sodas as they consumed an amalgam of soft rock, sultry pop and funk. They tapped their feet from Gladys through to the Dave Mason endings. Damien was glad to entertain in it all, something for which was a rarity at home. As soon as his grandmother and grandfather were in bed, so was he. The only way to recover the heat of the space, and of the joy of the nights before, was to make it echo with sound. He would surround himself with echoes.

Echoes could cushion if they were compact enough. A cushion that was as warm as the sleeping bag he had curled up in. He turned on the radio. A rock track pummelled out like a crowd, as communal as the atmosphere the radio could lend. With the radio there was someone else on the other side, it travelled like a body surfer staggering itself over the hands of a hundred people. It never dropped you because it never stopped, instead lowering you down gently as it smoothed its way into the next tune. And it had life because it was live through the air as though breathing itself into his room.

The sound made Damien feel alive. It shifted time and place away from the one he was in. Seven days ago was bad. But yesterday was good. Today started bad, but maybe he could end it good. His mind was a jumble. As confusing as the concept of a year having two meanings, two lives, two entries and two exits. When it started and when it finished. Could it run in duplicate until one caught up the other? Then he realised he forgot his birthday in that equation and the year made up of four parts – which was the season that started it then ended it? He wasn't sure when the end of the year was. Was tomorrow going to be better than today? He hoped so.

He flicked on his keyboard and started to muck about with various songs he had taught himself how to play. In the background the radio continued to oxygenate the room with its crowded breath, morphing itself into a makeshift backing track to the music he tapped out on the keys. Depending on the background's beat, he'd change the song. He'd tap his feet and bop his head and shoulders with the rhythm of the bass pulsating his body to a climate in opposition to the season. He mined the loftiness as though in a chase of the golden meteor[19].

Images dashed through his mind of the faces of who he wanted to be. If he could project himself on a screen on his bedroom wall, it would leak the rose of his blood speckled with the glitter of yolk from his soul where he could paint a border of black so he could keep it contained so if he ever needed to find it again it would always be there in the same spot, never lost. And the radio never lost its breath as it perforated itself through the room, jousting him into the next song as he nodded his head with accord.

He stopped for a moment to recompose his reverie and leaned across to turn the radio down to low. With the quiet in-between he could hear Jeanie's pseudo audience laugh, followed by the muffled chuckle of his grandmother. It made him think of the Midnight Special. The crowds' applause resounded like a deck of wooden cards falling from a height as it hit the ground. One audience was always going to be more powerful than another. One was going to generate more heat.

He turned the radio back up. He listened for where it was

---

[19] Verne, Jules. *The Chase of the Golden Meteor*. 1909. First English Edition. Grant Richards, London. Sourced from Golia, Maria. *Meteorite*. 2016. Reaktion Books.

deserving of his ear and deserving of his heart. Deserving of his applause. Were they giving him an Ace or giving him the Jack? He laughed. Every cadence was an Ace of Diamonds to him. He was just the hungry jackal scavenging for what they could feed him. To listen was something beyond his ear. It spread through every part of his body.

Then the power went out.

"Here we go again!" He heard Claudia denounce from the other room.

He looked out the window, the only place where the light was coming from, emitting through its watery thickness. The quiet brought back the chill. No-one would survive outside in that cold. He thought of Ava. *She wouldn't be out there by herself*, he reassured himself. It was too cold outside. It was too cold for him to go and look. Hummingbirds don't fly in a rain as heavy as the one out there. Anyway, it was the wrong season.

CHAPTER TWENTY-EIGHT

Damien hungrily eyed the Atari[20] joystick console at the electronics store. It was a pipe dream to think anyone might buy it for him. It was expensive, even as a birthday gift – a wish too painful to beseech when the question came of what he wanted. "Be considerate of what you ask for," Claudia had always said. "God isn't greedy and neither are you." It wasn't something he needed he told himself, a logic combatant with its desire. Nevertheless it made going into the store to play on the demonstration model an enticement in competition with the original reason he wanted to pay a visit.

As far as competition went, it spawned a new form. Patrick on occasion joined him sitting in the corner where Damien commanded first right of play (and replay), therefore by default owned the machine. An understanding that saw Patrick sit quietly and obey whatever order of play was instructed by his friend, given the occasional testiness of its player. And Damien liked to win, something not lost on his companion through many an arcade gaming session. But the comradery in which the two of them enjoyed made them a

---

[20] Atari® video game console, Atari, Inc (1972 – 1984).

transfixed pair well into the afternoon until the store closed. On one day the owner had to tap them both on the shoulder after the lights had already been switched off, like a security officer in the night having sprung them picking a lock. The owner didn't mind them being there. Sometimes Damien even showed customers how to use it.

That along with his curiosity in the TRS-80[21] lead to a discovery that he didn't think anyone else had found on the computer at school. The school had bought a computer and had introduced students to its use on a rotational basis in the library for word processing. He had read about the games that could be played on the TRS-80 in Popular Electronics[22] magazine becoming transfixed on what they could do, enthralled by the prospect that the Atari could be plugged into it too. It was easy to become engrossed, especially once he had found the Backgammon game on the machine in the library. During free periods he played Backgammon, under a cover of word processing, provided there was no-one else on it, or looking – as open to chance as the roll of a die. Shutting it down and then starting play all over again if anyone walked passed produced an irritation commensurate with losing to the opposing player. Interruptions from external forces were never good for play, equivalent to losing one's train of thought, therefore never arriving to the conclusion – to prove he could win.

The school librarian had come up to him one day sniffing him out. He'd seen her approaching out of the corner of his eye and had quickly exited the screen.

"Was that a game you were playing?" She nudged at him with a nosy countenance.

"No, no," he quipped. She glared at him in return in

---

[3] TRS-80° is a computer manufactured by the Tandy Corporation. 1977.

[22] Popular Electronics° Magazine. Ziff Davis Publishing Company. 1954-1982.

disbelief.

"I think I know what I saw."

"I don't think so," he innocently deflected back. She blinked at him. He could feel a hot rash trickle across his neck and in a fluster blurted out, "I was looking into the TRSDOS command line interface through the CPU cache." She just squinted at him. He didn't really know exactly what that meant either but knew that ought to do it. Popular Electronics had it covered. She walked away thoroughly confused leaving him be.

Why they had to buy the computer so close to when school was to end was beyond sense. He would have to wait three months before he could use it again. A major annoyance given he had gotten good at it. So his train of thought had to change with the summer that was trickling closer and faster than its lava heat. He quickly became aware of where he would spend every other day during it – the store.

He became singed on one of those days. Elyse, her brother and father had come into the store where he was taken quite unawares when they walked in and bought the Atari. Damien thought he had both died and gone to heaven when the store's owner asked him to show them how it worked. A stake through the heart of humiliation and cupid bliss wrapped him into such a state he developed the shakes and a burning red rash down his neck.

"Hi Damien." Elyse was the essence of sweet as she confidently said hello, like it didn't faze her in the least at seeing him.

"This is you're boy?" Elyse's father commented as he handed over the cash at the register.

"Almost, given the amount of time he spends here" the owner acknowledged.

"Well, here you go young man. Appreciate the help.

You're a true salesman." He slipped a one dollar note in front of Damien, which he gratefully accepted.

"Thanks," he smiled back surprised.

When they walked out the owner folded his arms. "Maybe you should clear out before I have to start paying you," he joked.

"Oh ok," Damien ushered a look toward the door.

He held his arm out to stop him and opened the till.

"Here," he gave him five dollars. "Spend it wisely." Damien's eyes lit up. "Go on, get out of here."

He rolled the notes up into a tube and batted it on the palm of his left hand like a drum stick on a soft skin as he sprung down the footpath. He bought fries and a milkshake and spent a dollar at the arcade. He retained the rest for a record he wanted to buy and with the pocket money from Frank he just slid into the affordability bracket. Then it was a day complete – *he* would be complete, he thought.

He cut through an alley down the back of the shops as a shortcut on the way to the music store. When he turned the corner, a couple of boys were huddled together on their bikes as Damien walked passed, momentarily halting, turning their heads at the moment they saw him. He knew who they were, he recognised them from school. They let out a splutter of illicit laughs, riled in a peculiar stupidity.

"Whoops." One boy blustered.

"Quick, hide it!" The other shot out with a smothered chuckle.

Damien eyed the brown paper bag enclosing a bottle and by deduction of their demeanour knew they were drunk. He just walked on but not fast enough to avoid catching their passing words.

"Don't worry, he's no-one." They chirped like chicks in a nest, before spluttering into giggles. Damien glanced at the brown paper bag. The boy caught his gaze, then wheeled his bike across in front of him cutting him off and knifed a death stare in Damien's face. It was a warning. Damien deflected it with an apprehensive flick of his eyes to the ground until the boy twisted the front of his wheel to let him pass. Damien didn't hesitate and quickened his pace. The boy stared at him and with a cutting undertone slipped out of his mouth: "Orphan". Then laughed.

Its subversive malevolence tripped Damien up with the thud of his soul and he halted and turned his head ever so slightly along with his eyes as he caught two glassy ones staring at him with a grin. He turned away and walked on with his head down.

He pulled open the door of the music store, it chimed its Rudolph bell. When he picked up the record he wanted, no matter how high he held it in front of him, an overwhelming sense of deflation engulfed. He paid the last of his money to the cashier as though for an unwanted gift. It was a reward for himself that he wanted, now tainted. He walked out of the door with an uneasy sensation as he ruminated in his head seething *why did I go that way*? He clenched his teeth and felt a sniggering sense of retribution for all the words he wanted to funnel out at them, *should* have pierced them back with. Damien was getting good with words, why didn't he have the nerve to bite back with a greater degree of cunning and spite he knew was within him. He walked back, taking a different route, as though with leaden bolts tied to his feet.

Damien stared down at the record in front of him, The Man-Machine, as he sat on the kerb waiting for the bus. The air had turned taciturn. The purchase was a moot point that muted the rest of the journey home with a sudden downbeat demeanour, a mood following the path of the setting sun.

He lay on his back on his bed with a poker face, as the

vinyl spun its circle. He closed his eyes as Neon Lights[23] played and imagined a cluster of colours in space above him, like atoms ignited as they bounced off one another. The Man-Machine[24] and Metropolis[25], so few words freed the need for any that had been said. The electronic pulse of instruments ran an ambience into the space. He opened his eyes and stared at the cover. Pale faces, pinched ties, skinny men in lipstick, and a red that was as consuming as the words that weren't there. He closed his eyes again. Its pace was fast – running, sprinting. He knew he could run. He could run really fast. Run the hell away from all of them fuckers.

[23] Hütter, Ralf & Bartos, Karl & Schneider, Florian & Schult, Emil. "Neon Lights" from the album *The Man-Machine*. Performed by Kraftwerk. Kling Klang / EMI Electrola. 1978.

[24] Hütter, Ralf & Bartos, Karl. "The Man-Machine" from the album *The Man-Machine*. Performed by Kraftwerk. Kling Klang / EMI Electrola. 1978.

[25] Hütter, Ralf & Bartos, Karl & Schneider, Florian. "Metropolis" from the album *The Man-Machine*. Performed by Kraftwerk. Kling Klang / EMI Electrola. 1978.

CHAPTER TWENTY-NINE

Dust had a certain scent when it was left untouched. It was staid. Uneventful. It seemed odd to him when it was swilled by Claudia's feathers after a clean, those same fibres when airborne took on a different olfactory smell. There was something sensible about leaving things as they were. Unrifled. Rifling scattered debris. But the more he sat still, the more he felt scattered. Like wanting to move when he couldn't.

He sat in front of the television flicking the channels, until he came to the commercials and watched them back to back. Then he changed the channel until he found another one with a commercial again. Any television show made him feel sick. But somehow there was comfort in a commercial, devoid of the static familiarities in television serials. The commercials were short, sharp, to the point – and they were constantly moving onto the next one. With happy slogans and niceties that made him feel better. Because they arrived and sustained with such brevity, when they were gone there was no sense of loss. Just moving, somewhere.

He had spent the previous hour bouncing a ball against the back shed, punching at it with the palm of his hand so hard it became sore. It was an endless pursuit of forceful reciprocation trying to keep the pendulum of time unstuck – to keep him from the tiring monotony of another day without much to do – to unstick him: a pendulum clock turned sideways[26]. Nothing to do bred too many thoughts that he wanted out of his head. He needed motion and the only way was to get out of the house. He switched the television off and grabbed his bike skidding off in the direction of Patrick's.

He found Patrick up the side of his house stacking firewood from the back of a trailer. He saw his father briefly before he disappeared into the house again.

"Hey," Damien called out, riding up close.

"Hi." Patrick looked up.

"You want to go play Space Invaders[27]?"

"I can't," he let slip despondently. "I have to unload this, then go back for a second load with Dad."

"Oh, ok," Damien nodded, twisting the wheel by the handlebars.

"Well, you can come if you want," Patrick offered.

Damien stopped for a second before responding. "That's ok." He turned his bike around. "I'll catch you later." And rode off back down the driveway.

He rode down to the main road, then took a left, followed by a right down a path through to the creek. He dumped his bike on the embankment thick with dying grasses in the dehydrated creek-bed and walked down to the water. It was strangely unnatural in its quietness, even in the stretches of light, like being in an abandoned playground. The quiet made

---

[26] Pendulum Clock analogy. From Feynman, Richard P. *Six Not So Easy Pieces*, copyright © 2001. Reprinted by permission of Basic Books, an imprint of Hachette Book Group, Inc.

[27] Space Invaders is an arcade game developed by Tomohiro Nishikado. Published by Taito. 1978

him too aware of it, of him being there alone. He used to like it here. Now the stillness made his body feel stagnant and stuck like a dead reed. He picked up a rock and threw it skimming it across the water. It bounced along its top like a frog, until he noticed it had nicked the edge of a boulder where a lizard clung and knocked it off. He half laughed under his breath at the strike. He saw another skink on an opposing rock. He picked up a small rock and slung it like a sling shot aimed directly beneath the lizard's perch and just at the tip of the water beneath it. It hit the boulder and water with a sloshing thud, then ricocheted upward and hit the skink who slipped straight underneath. He laughed and felt chuffed at his skill. *He was simply scaring sparrows for his own amusement*[28]. Such entertainment was as good a distraction as any compared to doing nothing at all.

He walked around to the boulder and saw the lizard floating belly up. He knelt down and scooped it up with his hand, resting its lifeless body gently against the rock at his feet, its silver belly up. It made a pulsating fit that propelled Damien back in fright, until it stopped moving altogether. He didn't know if it was really dead or just a tactic of play. Lizards were good at freezing when they sensed a predator. He picked up a nearby twig and flipped it over onto its stomach revealing its slender serpentine body. He peered down inspecting it closely, its brown-grey scales, more like a spongey mushroom than a reptilian dry skin. They were meant to be as old as the dinosaurs. He remembers the lessons of their evolution from classes, years before. How could something as old as the dinosaurs be so vulnerable to death? It seemed younger than him lying prostrate upon the

---

[28] " I was simply scaring sparrows for my own amusement". Dostoyevsky, Fyodor. *Notes from Underground*. Translated by Jessie Coulson. First edition. 1972 London: Penguin Red Classic. 2006. First Published as Zapiski iz Podpolya, Russia, 1864.

rock. Probably only one year old. Yet Damien was younger than its evolution. Maybe that was its paradox[29]. One had travelled faster than the speed of light through time, faster than the other. The thing that lasts longer is the thing that keeps moving. The lizard lasted longer because it never stopped. It knew how to detach and keep running. That made it younger than him compared to if he had just stood still through the course of time. That made it a survivor. Though, the end of this one's life was at his feet, relative to his point of view. He'd killed it. Yet he hadn't killed its evolution. If only he could kill the evolution of his own life that seemed to be going nowhere. Like a myth.

He tossed it back in the water and turned around to head up the embankment to his bike. Too much time gazing at things upon rocks was as idle as the time itself – he could pass it but couldn't capture it back. Damien had to keep moving. It was the only way he could last as long as he could – longer than the evolution of the baby lizard, before anyone could knock him down, writhing until he stopped altogether.

Boredom was the twisting, sinking, wriggling, niggling that turned itself into an internal thrashing – he just pedalled harder. The faster he rode, the more abundant the wind that swept into the back of his throat, cooling down its burning sensation with too much time to churn in angst. He paced his bike in a race with himself up and down the dirt road until it kicked up a dust storm as though from a turbine. Its deliberateness of execution evidenced by the pain in his thighs and chest. Even when he rode with the wind, he knew he could out-pace the storm chasing behind him. Even if it was a storm he had created.

But if storms were dust and dust was dirt, its sediment

---

[29] Chapter 4, s4.2 The Twin Paradox. From Feynman, Richard P. *Six Not So Easy Pieces*, copyright © 2001. Reprinted by permission of Basic Books, an imprint of Hachette Book Group, Inc.

always settled. Unless the forecast was windy with a chance of rain. He looked up. The sun was still high in the sky and bathed his face. There wasn't a cloud in sight. He stopped pedalling and came to a rest.

He realised the point at where he was and swiftly turned his head to the side noticing the fence post. The old decrepit post, where his humble fortress was once erected at its base festooned with dandelions. Now it resembled a pile of dilapidated rubble. Sticks and stones. *Why do they tell you that?* He thought, thinking of the things that made him crumble so easily, so physically. It was a lie along with everything else. Because everything hurt.

Maybe if he could bash at the things that hurt. Wrap them in a balloon of their hot air pasted with paper and punch at its piñata until it burst apart. The icing sugar coated words used to cover the stones would disintegrate as dust along with it. He looked away, trying not to think of the things he tried to build to protect himself, seeing them fall apart. The sun speared him the longer he was motionless, his black t-shirt vigorously absorbing its heat. He glanced upwards and squinted away just as quickly. Sunspots stained the path ahead of him, the consequence for those who dare catch a glimpse of something more powerful than them. The trick was not to look into the thing that burns.

He kicked up the dirt again with his tyre tread until he made his way home. Walking into his bedroom, the sunspots hadn't left him emerging stronger in the darkness of the room until they started to irritate. The wall above his bed was where they appeared the strongest blinking at him like eyes of owls in the night caught by reflected headlights. He wanted to punch at them with his fists to make them go away. They were as acute as the ringing in his ears after a symbol clap. He looked away with frustration toward the window – the only place that was always his means of escape.

The spots disappeared in the light.

CHAPTER THIRTY

His voice warbled and lilted and husked. To Claudia it was like a duckling who had lost his feathers. In Frank it produced a broad grin. Any time he heard Damien talk whenever it hit a sudden baritone rollercoasterd from an upper inflection he slung out his hand in front of Damien in a handshake.

"Put it there Master," he gave him a stern pat on his shoulder as he struck out his hand. "Any hairs on your chest yet?" He joked.

Claudia fussily shook her head at him. "Stop it Frank, don't embarrass the boy."

Damien smirked in response and stared at his plate of food to distract himself, somehow sucking up the red from a sweet potato as it kissed his cheeks. He couldn't hide from this and it was irreversible and they couldn't possibly know how he felt. He forked at the food on his plate. The food tasted the same as the year before, it felt the same in his mouth and as he swallowed. But this thing in his throat was changing. A peculiarity that was normal, but made him feel anything but. If he had breathed in hard in the icy air outside would it slow the process down or speed it up? The thought hurt his throat.

One thing was for certain it could mark the perfect exit from the Christmas choir. He put it to his grandmother mildly.

"Well, yes I suppose you are old enough to make that choice if that's what you want. Barbara will be very sad to see you go. She always enjoyed having you in it."

Barbara had always treated him carefully, as though having him there was beyond special, which he had learned to use to his advantage in the front row position in which he tried to place himself until her attention was all consuming and he cagily tried to avoid her. He understood her attentiveness but when it wasn't wanted it always left him feeling somewhat inadequate, as though he was her community service announcement, or prize not for her taking – he wasn't sure which.

Church bred an awkward sense of all eyes being on him, of hidden whispered looks that had never abated, making him uncomfortable. Here, there were no secrets. He railed at their beliefs. He didn't want to be around them. Faced with another barrage of eyes and opinions, it became a place he was so desperate to avoid or suffer in silence praying for its social activity to end. He craved to be alone somewhere where no-one knew a thing.

He'd sung so many hymns and carols and stood angelic by his grandmother's side all his life. He didn't know how much longer he could stand in a pew anymore, let alone sing in front of a congregation of worship he didn't follow, feeling like he was in a parody ensemble with a manacle chained to a ball bearing. If he didn't detach from it, he would explode. So this minor alteration to festivities thanks to the breaking of his internal chords was the angel on top of the tree. He'd fly off it free.

If angels were to swoop, they soon were to scatter their fairy dust like desiccated coconut. He looked up from his plate outside the dining room window, where the porch light glistened itself into the evening. The only thing flying free were the leaves, making their final copper descent leaving bare black skeletons, where they dug their claws into a grass still green with moss at their roots. He imagined the stems of the leaves as the broken strings of the angel's harp making whirligigs from their glowing filament as they fell. He wondered what broken strings sounded like as they fell through air. If they slapped against the black skeletons could they spring them back to life, not wait until they mulched into the earth to feed them at their feet. Broken strings couldn't stop it metamorphosing like him. Claudia broke his gaze.

"Make sure you tell her in good time, so she knows."

"I'll let her know next week."

"Any plans for something else?" Frank asked.

"Maybe." He guardedly offered as he played with the snake beans drowning in the gravy on his plate.

He thought of the strings that made the harpsicord and how it came to be as the keyboard. Strings of guitars, a keyboard and the sound of a drum were all he could think of and the ensemble he wanted to join where he was more eager to commit his attention than to the chorales of cherubs. In less than a year he would be out of Junior High. Senior was where he could join it. He'd seen the band play. That was the congregation he really wanted to be in. At least there would be no more early morning wake ups to attend pre-church practise. He had started to find it harder and harder to get up in the morning, feeling more like a sloth in the bed on the weekend having a stronger desire for longer sleep. He just told himself it was a sign he was meant to work the other way around – wakeful at night and sleep during the day. That is how he felt he was wired. He listened to music long into the night, playing it low close to his ear, where he invariably fell asleep to it. It bred a new noise for the night. He decided to park these night-time daydreams.

He excused himself from the table and took his plate to the kitchen. Rinsing it under the tap, he could see the silver scratch marks upon the white ceramic from years of purpose – that which sustains and keeps you alive. Each pencil lead-like mark represented a point in time, a night somewhere back in his memory that couldn't be cleaned away. The marks of his childhood. For a brief second it splashed back the image of the blonde haired boy with the sunny disposition, a commercial of the cute and sweet and clean. Children left stains. Didn't they realise that? There was nothing clean about them. A fabrication by someone with something to sell. Like detergent. It made him suddenly feel vindicated he would truly be leaving the chirping cherubs in the past.

As he turned around to walk out, Ava was leaning against the wall.

"I didn't realise you were here. Where have you been?" He said in passing.

She gave him a curious look. "You sound funny. What happened to your voice?"

"It broke," he said.

"Oh."

He walked down the hall to his bedroom and turned on the radio. He didn't need Ava thinking of him as oddly as he thought of himself. He closed the door behind him.

CHAPTER THIRTY-ONE

Dreams have a strange way of inverting themselves. When they become nightmares. It was two nights before he was due to return to school and in a semi consciousness he could hear himself beat out "fuck them" under his breath as he woke thrashing in a state of distress under the sheets. He had been playing The Man-Machine all day and its red had played on his mind, reminding him of that day, even in its miles away. He lay in bed with his hands to his head with an intensely sickening disdain and revolt. Two weasels. Unable to rid his mind of them with any day he saw them in school. He wished he had spat on them back then and there. But he was no Ponyboy and there was no Johnny to drag him out of the fountain.[30] He was neither. He didn't know what he was. Yellow. He didn't fight. *I can fight you. Fuck you.* With their pudgy little faces mottled red, their glassy eyes and liquored lips he wanted to punch them. He detested their faces. He had seen them in the street again on their bikes a week ago. They couldn't help the way they were. Brains like mushed up

---

[30] References from Hinton, S.E. *The Outsiders*. 1967. First Edition. The Viking Press. Published in Penguin Classics 2007.

peas, like the sniggering vomit coming out of their mouths. The thoughts of them propagated as though watered with acid and putrefied. Or was it his brain on the turn, rotting like a piece of fruit.

He turned down the sheets and walked to the bathroom to have a drink of water. He captured his face in the mirror through squinting eyes in the bright bathroom light, snapped on after darkness. His hair askew, a blotchy face, half awake, his eyes puffy with tears in which he wasn't sure if they were just from the light. He clenched his teeth and clamped his jaw wanting to scream. He held his hands to his head, to stop the tears from falling, its pressure too much to bear. He hastily splashed cold water on his cheeks. It was icy from the pipes and made them sting like needle pricks. No amount of its anaesthetic was enough to remove their bite marks on his brain.

He didn't need a Johnny he told himself. *I don't need anyone. So fuck you.*

He walked back to bed. With the sheet lain open the cold had gotten to it. It was like slinking into a sleeping bag that had been used to chill bottles. He waited for the thoughts to subside together with the cold, until he had warmed himself again. The closer the object the more detailed or sharp it appears. They were a long way away. But they remained in his line of sight, it just made the perspective skewed. He could make them far away where their proportion was small, where he was bigger than them and they were a mere spec. *I am better than you.* He could tread on ants.

He wandered his eyes about his head. He thought of the cute girl he saw at the corner store. Wandering eyes that didn't wander back at him. He'd taken a left to buy an ice cream instead. For all the cents he could collect for all the eyes looking elsewhere he'd be a rich man, he said to himself.

What's the use of a jar full of coins? They hold no true value. He needed paper. Like a dollar bill. He could roll it up or cut a few out in a line like a player. He was just missing the rock that would be the weight atop his growing mound.

He rolled over and tried to go back to sleep. All he could feel was the sweat of his anger. He sweat in the winter under the flannel sheets as though burning in fever. He flung the sheet off him inviting the ice back in to cool him down, only to wrap it back. Hot. Cold. External forces didn't know what he wanted, neither did he. He stared at the ceiling, then closed his eyes. Maybe if he lay flat on his back his brain might think different things. The pictures in his mind shifted depending on which way he lay. Some things were sharper if the pressure was on his left versus his right, or was it that it just relaxed his right versus his left. He didn't want them sharper, he wanted them gone. Lying flat was like walking straight across a pedestrian crossing, its zebra stripes mapped a grid of predictability. There was only one way. All or nothing. His *all* was that he was going to smear their image, until they were nothing but hazy faces.

He thought of Mary Jane and cocaine. He'd read the stories in music magazines of all his beloved stars and their apparent beloved vices. He wondered if they took it in order to make hazy faces of all the people in front of them, around them, following them, consuming them. Maybe they needed to consume something to block something out. There was always something to blot out. He was sure they must suffer. Maybe they suffered like him. One does not need a vice if one does not suffer? But his idols looked too stoic and strong to be sufferers. Maybe they took it to have fun. Boy did they look like they were having fun. It's what made him have his first taste.

If he joined the band in high school, he wondered if they smoked Mary Jane, as he did. *They looked too clean cut.* But then again Patrick's brother looked pretty neat most of the time and he was the one keeping him in supply after Patrick found a spliff one day during a cigarette pilfering sweep. He could feel a smile grace his face. Hazy faces looking up at an idol.

"What are you thinking about?" Ava softly spoke through the strange air.

"Guess." He calmly proffered after a beat, opening his eyes calmly.

"I don't know. You have gone quiet. You don't talk much anymore."

Damien lay on his bed and didn't say anything. Ava was sitting at his desk with her head resting on her hand rolling a glass paper weight back and forth watching its snowflake interior scatter within it, visible from the light of the stars outside.

"I don't mean to be. It's just the way I am," he dispersed.

Sometimes his head was crammed with a thousand things to tell her, such that it was too much and wedged like a barge at the gates. Sometimes his mind was empty, devoid of anything with too much of everything else jamming the rest out.

"You're stuck." She said.

He turned his head to her and looked at the glass roll under her palm.

"And you're scared. Scared to leave, scared to stay." She continued proliferating the air with the sweetness of her suggestions as to how he was. He liked her suggestions – sometimes.

"I don't know. Anyways, I'm going to play music. Music is my angel of exit."

"That's good huh."

A smile beamed upon his face at the thought.

"It will be the best thing ever." He let out a long-held

breath.

"What are you going to play?" She smiled.

"Everything."

"Can I come watch you play?"

"Yeah, you can come and watch me." He turned his head back to stare at the ceiling and imagined all the people who he might play to. He thought he would like Ava there. Wondered what she would think. The thought scared him as much as it thrilled.

"Do you think that is what you will do after you finish school?" She asked.

"Maybe. I don't know. There are too many things I want to do."

College was still a long way off and the thought of it was unsettling. Too many options became a tangle in his head – what if he picked the wrong thing? What if he was doing it for the wrong reason – to satisfy someone else? That only left a constricted set of options he didn't want to contemplate. But he resolved with himself he would do it his way. She was right. He was stuck.

"Just do it all," she whimsically breathed into the room.

Yeah, just do it all. He rolled over to the side table and switched on the radio with the volume down low, letting its music stretch in the small space between them, keeping the nightmare out.

CHAPTER THIRTY-TWO

A globule of blood plopped out upon the steel tray. He flicked his scalpel at the artery where a raisin size clot snagged itself upon the tip. He wiped it clean. The heart of an ox, its hugs and kisses were all back to front as it lay slain upon the biology lab table. Twelve ceased heartbeats scattered around the room with hungrily inquisitive pairs of eyes upon them. Damien made the first cut, skirting a trim like white lace, while Buttercup his lab partner manoeuvred her fingers in to prise the slit to reveal the arterial caverns.

"Go ahead, stick your fingers inside," the teacher insisted with a jest of dare.

Damien stuck his finger inside one of the holes while Buttercup held it open. It felt like a tight canal once flowing with a molten honey that had been left on its walls as residue. He wondered if that is what it felt like sticking a finger into the stacked polygons in a beehive. But for the strength of its oxen heart, it felt soft and spongey. He switched turns with Buttercup and he pulled it apart in his hands for her to see. With the whole of it in his hands it didn't feel as intricate as its covert interior. But with the whole he felt its weight.

If it was exsanguinated and sucked dry of all its blood,

cried of all its waters, all that would be left was carbon. That's all it was, the same as the earth underfoot. Whether it would be compact and hard, or whether it disintegrated as ash crushed between hands, he wasn't sure. He wondered what happened to the burning hearts of Seraphs, as they could never be turned to ash. Their burning could never be doused, not even by a rain of their own vapour. They existed too far up high in the sky, like in a white hole where only their light escaped, from which no-one could enter but them. Untouchable.

Damien cupped the heart back together, where it recuperated itself lying in a semi-distorted shape in front of them, patiently without escape, as though in sympathy for its aggressors. They put down their implements. They picked up the silver tray and tipped the heart into the bin as the teacher's assistant walked passed. They wiped the bench clean.

He found a seat outside. Recess brought a change in his demeanour with a sharp abruptness when he found himself without a partner. A solitary session seated on a steel bench in the quad started a sickness that was hard to get rid of until the bell rang and class returned. Class resumed his engagement on something important, rather than the inattention of wild thoughts that dashed about his brain waiting on a barge. He awkwardly shifted on the bench when anyone walked passed, furrowing his face further into the island of Prospero[31], feeling a freak for trying to interpret the script. A freak within a swarm. A freak that made him weigh them all up and cut them all down – as they passed.

Be wise as thou art cruel;" So an old sonnet goes, one he remembered.

---

[31] From Shakespeare, William. *The Tempest*. 1610-11.

He felt different from all of them. And he knew why. When exterior circumstances become interiors. He felt like a mule of his family. If only he could build a contraption that could cart the heavy weight of it in his place, freeing the load of its pain. 'It' had never left him and was slowly growing worse as time went on. He didn't know how to get rid of its niggling intrusion. He didn't have the power.

A blank page stared up at him from his lap, as he rested on his bed with his back against the wall back home waiting for dinner to be ready. He twirled his pencil in his hand and started to sketch pictures within the white frame. He drew a heart and coloured it charcoal and connected it with a string slipped out of the arm of a stick-figured boy, giving him a caption: *I lost my heart; the wind came to take it away.* He continued to draw up at the top of the page a UFO, the Death Star[32]™, and a space creature that looked like Godzilla[33], flanked by aliens finishing it off with a cluster of stars and a headstone that read RIP. Then he wrote out its eulogy. It tumbled out of him without thinking.

> *If I could take it away*
> *I'd take it tomorrow*
> *If I could rewind the day*
> *I'd kill all your sorrow*
> *If I could paint out the grey*
> *I'd paint you a rainbow*

---

[32] The Death Star™ as featured in Star Wars®. Created by George Lucas. 1977. Lucasfilm Ltd, Twentieth Century Fox.

[33] Godzilla from film Godzilla. 1954. Produced by Toho Co. Ltd. Created by Tomoyuki Tanaka, Ishirō Honda, Eiji Tsuburaya.

If I could stop my decay
I'd build me a scarecrow
To scare all the evil around me away

Damien occupied two rooms. One was with the person he wanted to be with. The other was with the person he wanted to get away from. One was the boy he wanted to help. The other was the boy he wanted to bury. The boy who wanted to make rain to wash away the boy who was sticking pins into himself – or was that in other people? Like an axe swung fast to split a piece of wood, it swung too hard and jammed inside the stump beneath, revealing a terrible reality – it only takes one swing to split you apart and jam you forever. It wasn't a hopscotched luck of the draw. It was one bold manoeuvre, one action that did it. The axe was the evil and he was starting to notice too many people reflected in its metal.

Claudia called out from the living room. The smell of pastry crust and buttery garlic permeated the house. It relaxed the muscles in his throat and awoke his stomach. It was familiar. It was the smell of warmth. And it chased things away, better than any rain. If home was where the heart was, then it was Claudia who had his heart. Maybe that was where it went, he lent it to her for his protection, without realising it. When the time was right he could ask for it back. He just didn't know when that would be.

CHAPTER THIRTY-THREE

The maples surrounded with a luminous emerald around the music hall as Damien sat on the step outside in the afternoon reading a book. He was waiting for everyone to arrive to open the doors for band practise. He could feel the cold concrete through the seat of his pants. He closed his book and stood up, feeling the back of himself. Spring seeped into itself from winter, leaving the steps damp. He should have known better surrounded by a scent of leafy compost. He pulled his sweater off and tied it round his waste to let it hang down behind him. But the air held onto its dampness too, where he could feel the afternoon chill through the sleeves of his jersey t-shirt. The teacher sprung up the steps, with a couple of students behind him.

"Good to see you! You ready?" The teacher beamed as he fumbled the keys through the lock.

"Ready as I'll ever be."

"That's the spirit."

The hall was almost as cold, but with the small group of them in the room, taking their positions, the warm-up rounds ignited the air, like the heat from a sparkler gently proliferating the space. They launched into some soul starting with Stevie Wonder's Superstition[34]. Damien sat and watched, completely aware they may be watching him. He had started to inject an implied enthusiasm in the presence of others as he carefully gauged their reciprocation. He'd learnt to read people's faces and could tell the genuineness lay embedded in a person's eyes. Here sitting in front of them he was their sole audience, where he could assess their movement and skill. To him, he wondered if they would do the same. It was for their graduation concert coming up in less than two months. This was the band he wanted to be in and the teacher had invited him to watch them rehearse and had asked him to show them how well he played. He had practiced two songs religiously for the last two weeks in order to show them he was qualified.

His heart sank with an abundance of nervousness when they stopped their final number and summoned him to the floor. Through the duration of the first song, he could feel the palpitations of his heart beating vigorously in his chest. But after the first song he played was over he felt a centrality to his core, more confident he could deliver what he was there to do. He ended it rumbling out his own modern rendition of Fats' Ain't Misbehavin'[35] with a back beat. He looked around the room of faces after he finished anxiously hoping for their approval.

"I think we could do with you joining us Damien." The teacher said. "You cut a mighty fine form on those keys."

He'd passed. The five players walked up and shook his hand. Gary played the drums, a girl called Mandy played the

---

[34] Wonder, Stevie. "Superstition" from the album *Talking Book*. Motown. 1972.

[35] Waller, Thomas "Fats" & Razaf, Andy & Brooks, Harry. "Ain't Misbehavin" from *Connie's Hot Chocolates*. 1929.

Sax, Peter played the bass and Dean was on guitar. He knew a couple of them through church and older siblings of friends in his class. But it was a group of people otherwise unknown. Tom played keyboards and was about to graduate from high school, so luck was on Damien's side – the spot was available - and he was it.

"So, you'll be here for next time we hope," Dean enthused at Damien.

"Yeah for sure." He cut back in nervous excitement.

"Just don't let Mandy drown you out with her brass," Tom joked giving Mandy a playful stare.

Mandy turned to him with a glare, flicking her chestnut hair over her shoulder "says you who turns the volume up max when you play the organ mode like you're in a cathedral."

Tom shrugged in response.

Damien took in their banter, hoping he was joining a group of people where fun was in abundance, rather than sledges to intimidate.

"Just don't play organ mode full stop. We want less grandma and more funk right?" Peter cut through all of them.

"Too right brother," Gary added. "Given what you just played now, you strike me as more funk than feline, right?" Gary bent like a beanpole turned to Damien.

"Yeah, anything with a beat." He said. "But I am happy to play anything."

"And that you will," Tom nodded at him knowingly.

They seemed a mismatched lot. Mandy in a cable knit beside Peter who was built like a bull flanked by Gary lithe like a weed. Dean was too clean cut for guitar, *not a patch on me*, Damien felt relieved.

He walked out of the hall with a feeling of pride equivalent to a small glimmer from a sparkler glowing red in a spot before it burst into a second coming, not yet at the end of its wire. This is what he had always wanted, always dreamed of. He'd spent so many nights watching bands on television and had seen this one play in front of home crowds and school assemblies. He wanted to be part of it, and now he was going to be. It was the first sense of joy he had in a long time, like a popping candy set off in a pond.

"You got a light kid?"

The scratchy voice of a man breathed past his shoulder as he walked outside the hall. Damien turned around. A hand waved out at him as reddened as frost bite, with a cigarette awaiting its fate between fingertips. A stench of his spirit seeped into the air between them like fumes from a bowser. Damien could see a tattoo of an eagle on his arm, its wings just visible under the sleeve of his jacket. People about the town called him Driller. He spent much of his time hanging around the steps of public establishments.

"No," Damien looked at him in the face quickly with a forward motion to keep moving, his smile disappearing just as swiftly. *Don't go near him* he remembered being told once when he was a kid.

That one quick look was enough to stain Damien's eyes. He had never been up this close to him before. Skin like ruddy red leather and eyes like a cracked pomegranate, blood blistering its white till they were white no more. The war outside had soaked into his head, where the munitions were as loud as the feet on the path walking passed him, pretending he wasn't there. But Damien didn't pretend he wasn't there. He couldn't forget those eyes. Damien continued walking ahead and was already several yards down the road by the time he turned around to see if he was still back in the parking lot. Damien continued home. He didn't know why they feared him. He'd gone on his way unhindered. The exchange would be his secret. *'He suffered all the stabs of all the killer crows*[36].' Crows perched up in sycamore trees where they hovered - watching. You'd never know when they swooped to peck at you. And they were always there, even in invisibility. The inconspicuous bird that radiates gloriousness on its perch, in its hiddenness could harm you. Like the valour of the badge still pinned to his breast.

Pride was to be honoured when hard work was at its core, but pride had a way of decimating a man through no fault of his own, for an unfortunate turn or for an honour that was serving someone else. *I'm not going to be serving anyone*, Damien concluded in his head. And no-one was going to take away the sense of accomplishment it was going to give him.

He rang John as soon as he got home to tell him the good news. There he could hear his voice down the end of the line confirming the reward of his work as deserved.

"I can't wait to see you play."

It was enough and it was all he wanted to hear.

He didn't ring Cynthia. He didn't want to speak to her. If he had to wait to deserve something, then she would wait to earn the right to know what was happening in his life. He would wait for her to come to him. He knew how this game worked now. She had created the rules. Now he knew how to make new ones to break hers.

---

[36] Baudelaire, Charles. A Voyage to Cythera; *The Flowers of Evil* Translated by James McGowan. First Edition. Oxford University Press. 1993. First published as *Fleursdumal*, France, 1857.

CHAPTER THIRTY-FOUR

He cracked an egg into the frying pan. Its sizzle in the hot butter plucked into the kitchen like the tap dance from the webbed feet of a duck. Its frying smell was sensational. He'd risen early to make his own breakfast ahead of a day trip into the city with Patrick. He had told Claudia he was going to look at keyboards at a music store. For the two of them, it would be a slight deviation. He scoffed down the egg with a piece of toast before grabbing his jacket heading off on his bike.

They rode to the train station, dumped their bikes and hopped on the city express service. The city with its gothic spired towers and rows of buildings stacked like cigars awaiting the flame of the night, sitting dormant casting their soft shadows in the morning's eastern light. The air had a crispness like camphor after rain on concrete underfoot. It was last night's party spilled as Semillon on the street.

Once inside the hidden walls the aroma changed. The theatre smelt of burnt popcorn oil and had a rank heavy mustiness. They sat in its cloistered darkness for the matinee session, with popcorn and Cokes® balanced on their laps, with a curious anticipation the moment the red curtain gathered itself back to reveal the cinema screen. Patrick's brother had already seen it and they knew they were in for something grim.

The screen slowly exposed the stacked arms of its title's letters, half there, half missing, for you to decipher like an acronym until it bore its name. From there on in the both of them were transfixed. The thing foreign creeped to then explode in fits, to resume a subdued calm until it crashed like a wave of shocking terror. A heartbeat skipped a hundred times over and an explosion in space to render it to oblivion saw it to its end. Damien sat there with his popcorn largely untouched passed the middle of the film.

They emerged from the cinema house into the bright stark light of day, relieved to abandon the darkness behind them and the new form of creature that may infest their consciousness.

"God damn, that was intense." Damien let out slightly rattled.

"Hell yeah."

"Man..." Damien trailed off without knowing what to say. They just kept walking like they needed to get the hell out of there.

As they passed a convenience store, Damien held his hand out to Patrick to halt him.

"Hey wait up." He pulled out five dollars and held it in front of Patrick. "Here, can you go buy a packet of smokes?"

Patrick looked at him awkwardly. "Why do I have to do it for?"

"You look older." He looked at Patrick pleadingly. "I'll give you five of them." He coerced.

Patrick grabbed the cash summoning the courage to befit the task assigned. "Fine."

"And a lighter," he whispered after him as he walked into

the store. Damien nervously waited on the kerb. A lady with a pram walked passed as Patrick emerged with a look as though he had just committed a robbery and as soon as Damien saw the packet and lighter in his hands he exclaimed in understated elation that still hadn't left him since walking out of the theatre.

"Right on!" They both scurried out of view of the shop front.

They had half an hour to spare before the train departed. The offer of time was too much to bear negotiating what to do with it.

"Do you want one?" Damien pulled out a cigarette from the packet, then motioned them both to walk to a side spot away from anyone's view and leant against a back wall in a side alley. He pulled out a second one for Patrick and offered the first strike of the lighter. This time they knew how to do it properly. They breathed in hard. They breathed out in half-coughs until their throats felt the smoke's sand paper graze. Whether it helped calm their nerves or add to their shakes it didn't much matter – it was the perfect distraction.

"They smoked on the Nostromo[37]," Patrick noted.

"Did you notice the robot – he didn't smoke. If they had noticed that they might have figured things out a bit earlier on." Damien contributed.

Patrick nodded. "But not everyone smokes. I can't remember if he ate anything. That would have been a clue."

"All the singers smoke." Damien added.

Between the two of them they rattled off all the names of all the singers they knew who smoked.

"Like Morrison." Patrick offered.

"Reed."

---

[37] From the film *Alien* Brandywine Productions. Twentieth Century Fox. 1979.

"Henley."

"Hendrix."

"And Cash."

"Hmm..." Damien concluded in acknowledgement.

Given it was just about every one of them, they pondered whether it was a more intriguing exercise to consult the names of those who didn't.

"It makes your voice sound better." Damien asserted. "That's why they do it."

"Well then why are you smoking? You don't sing. You play keyboards." Patrick half mocked.

"Because it's cool. Don't question it." Damien gave Patrick a friendly punch. "Anyway, maybe I will do both."

Patrick raised his eyebrows in a 'fair enough' gesture as he raised his cigarette and took a final drag.

"But they all smoke Mary Jane." They both nodded at each other knowingly – if only they knew where they could buy *that* right now. Some things required a little digging. "How's your brother these days?" Damien turned to Patrick in daring.

Patrick got the gist of the question and punched Damien in the shoulder playfully. "He's fine." Half wishing he'd never told Damien of his discovery that day hidden within his brother's packet of cigarettes.

Damien gave him a look with his eyebrows raised awaiting the rest of the answer he wanted. Patrick gave him a playful look and shook his head, before putting the butt out under his foot.

"We had better head off," Patrick suggested.

"One last thing." He looked down at his watch. "We've got time if we are quick." He urged.

To relieve his admission to Claudia, Damien dragged

Patrick with him to the piano store. He wasn't going to leave without checking out the polyphonic synthesiser he had read about in Musician[38] magazine. He owned his own 61 key electronic keyboard, but never formally played a synthesizer.

The store had a row of Roland® and Yamaha® keyboards amongst others and a few synthesisers including a Mellotron® which Damien had his heart set on. Damien had visited the store not that long ago. He hadn't been back since and was itching to check out the synths, because no-one had one like these in town.

"Can I help you?" A young man walked up to him as he stared curiously at the synths in front of him.

"Um, just looking." Damien politely noted.

"You play?" The sales assistant asked in a friendly banter.

"Yeah, well, not one of these, but maybe one day."

The sales assistant pressed the "on" switch and placed his finger on one of the keys, winding a knob on the top box. "You can adjust the tone and layer different samples and filter sounds. Gives you different resonance." He watched on with keen interest. "Here have a play around."

Damien stepped in front of it and played a few notes, gently turning the wheel and knob on the box. "Which one is the amplifier?" he asked.

"Here," the young man pointed to the plug connecting the amp, then turned a couple of knobs. "Choose the pitch you want to emphasise. Can give you a nice fat sound." Damien pressed down a key and manoeuvred the controls. "Yeah, that's it. You've got it. It's sensitive to how soft or hard you touch too." The sales assistant demonstrated softly touching the key, then hitting it swiftly. Its change in hardness of sound bounced back at them.

---

[38] Musician magazine founded by Sam Holdsworth and Gordon Baird. 1976 – 1981.

"Cool," Damien nodded his head impressed. He could have stayed there for hours, but they had to get back before too many questions were asked as to where they had been for so long. Patrick was loitering around the organs like a baby antelope as Damien turned around to see where he was.

"Thanks for the demo," Damien acknowledged.

"Sure, no problem. Hope you get a chance to play it for real one day."

On the way out he saw a poster for a rock concert pinned to a board on the wall. The band was one he liked and he would have died to go. But it was too far away to come at night by themselves. He just stared at the poster in awe. A couple of them in the picture held lazy cigarettes between their fingers in a casual nonchalance to match their stares. Maybe there was a way he could get there.

As the train shuttled itself over the tracks, the thudding of its heavy metal made him drift back to over a year ago when John took him to see his first rock concert. He could have closed his eyes to take himself back there, but they glazed over in the scene of countryside out the window. The rows of curated crops were like patterns placing him into a trance. The railway track churn transported him. The lights had been spectacular. The sound had been even bigger on that night, like a thunder rebounding off the theatre's walls in its containment in the dark. Nothing like what he experienced of the performances in town. True concerts amplified with a bass that pulsated through the floor through his whole body, pumping him with every kick of the drum. And it was the faces. Everybody's faces in the dark. They said it all – eyes glued – to the one thing on the stage. He had to be there. *One day*, he said to himself. *One day*. His eyes sewed the seed, and something internal manifested within. This is what he wanted to do. He didn't know how to convince the people he needed to in order to make it happen.

For all the high regard everyone paid to his music, they held the highest regard to his studies. He had slipped back a grading in one of his subjects that caused his grandfather to hound him on the importance of its place in securing a future for himself.

"Focus on your maths and science. They are what will get you places." Frank asserted to him over the dinner table one night.

Cynthia had barrelled him up the day before when she saw him on the weekend. She had said exactly the same phrase. They must have been talking about him behind his back. The thought made him shudder.

"Yes of course." He replied as he stared at the pepper shaker. How to convince any one of them of what he really wanted seemed impossible, so he just kept his desires to himself. More than anything, he hated that they talked behind his back. Living between households created a stream of additional lines of communication that he wished he could intercept, so he knew exactly what was going on, what was being said and by whom. He knew the pattern of decision making made in the past without his consultation and he deeply resented them all for it. Tell someone one thing and it came back via someone else with a new set of commands that he wasn't interested in receiving in the first place. It made him feel like a pawn, presided over and jostled. He was sure Rory was getting away scot-free.

"We'll make a doctor out of you yet." Claudia smugly joked. It was a joke that actually made Damien laugh for the mere fact he knew he would rather kill something than heal it. Maybe she knew him better than anyone.

CHAPTER THIRTY-FIVE

Ava's arms had grown slender like the curved muscle of a gentle sand dune. She was looking progressively long and lean, from Damien's point of view. He worried she had grown taller than him. He would check next time he stood next to her. Today she was leaning against his desk as he was trying to get through his homework. She kept squiggling conjoined with plus signs all around the borders along with = e in a glyph star-like flick around the corners of his exercise book. He half wondered if she knew what it meant, half annoyed she was contaminating his page.

"You're messing up the page," he said crankily.

"I'm only trying to help." She withdrew.

"How are you helping?" He asked irritated.

"Ask me a question and I'll give you the answer." She shot back.

He narrowed his eyes at her. "I know the answers." He rebutted.

"Suit yourself." She put the pen down.

She sat at his keyboard and started to play. It wasn't switched on so all he heard was the sound of the clicking keys.

"I know you'd rather be playing this." She sighed.

Damien made a huff. *YES, I KNOW THAT!* He wanted to shout at her. His wish had come true and he'd gotten all the things he wanted to do that he'd now swamped himself with them. What he needed was to have her out of the room.

"Don't you have a Barbie doll to go play with or something?"

Ava squinted back at him at the condescension and stood up with her adolescent frame towering over him sitting in his chair, when her eyes caught his windowsill.

"I prefer cars," she plucked back at him as swiftly as she plucked a matchbox variety off the sill and walked out of the room.

If there was a balance of forces to be as opposed as the power they wrought, Ava was a force whose pressure was starting to tip a scale in a direction he didn't like. A charm bracelet lightly scattered with jewels, now heavy with the confidence of her growing wisdom. It ingratiated especially at times when his patience was already being tried. A patience he was starting to discover he didn't have. *I know more than you do* was what he wanted to tell her. It was an acknowledgement for which his recipient had delved into head first, to delve into his brain for all he knew. It was a prophecy that was to change it. *She knows too much.* The thought irritated him, as much as the equations all over his page. He ripped out the page and re-wrote what he had written. All the answers all over again.

Wars were like long silences or was it that long silences were like wars. He wanted her there, then he didn't. She said all the right things, until she said too much. When she was gone he wouldn't think of her until he started to wonder where she was. If only she knew exactly how she should be, then it would work out ok, he told himself. If she could learn, then she could stay for as long as she liked. *She could be the ideal, didn't she know that?* He grew frustrated. He didn't know what she was to him and was perturbed by her superciliousness to walk out.

He grabbed his sweater and went out of the house. Late afternoon's chill rankled his knuckles as he rode his bike over to Patrick's who was watching Bandstand[39] when he arrived. Damien joined him on the floor in front of the television. He was indifferent to the show. They didn't play much of what he liked. The look of the happy teens dancing around made him view them as feral, worse than any freak he had been called, to his mind anyway. This wasn't the new wave he was wanting to fly over the top of. He preferred the late night music shows, which Claudia and Frank now let him watch from time to time. His engagement with this screen wavered.

"Hey, you're brother around?" He asked Patrick and pulled out some dollars from his trousers.

Patrick looked at the tufts of cash carefully placed under his nose. He shuffled on the floor in discomfort.

"You can't keep making me buy your stuff." Patrick urged the money back with his eyes. "The person in the next room, well that's my mother and she found two spliffs in my pocket from the last time and grounded me for the weekend."

Damien shrugged his shoulders. "But it's your brother who buys them." Damien pleaded with his eyes. "You smoke them too, what's the big deal?"

Patrick made a quiet huff. "You've got to buy it yourself some time." Patrick picked up the cash mildly disgruntled, forever his loyal servant.

Damien hid his smile beneath his hands. The girls on the

---

[39] Bandstand refers to the music TV show *American Bandstand*. Dick Clark Productions & WPVI-TV & ABC. 1964-1981.

TV were swinging their hips to a romantic number. *Ah, girls or spliffs?* He pondered the thought for a brief moment. *Girls and spliffs. I can get me a girl anytime*. Just not right now. He plucked himself off the floor to head back home. He wanted to play his own records and think of the contraband soon to be passing his lips. Sweet collateral held in the hands of his friend. He knew he delivered, he always did.

Lying on his bed back home, he wondered what it was like to blow a smoke kiss with a girl. He had seen it done in the movies. Was it sweeter when you were the one sucking in or the one blowing out? It was a job left to the experts. He was sure he would try it one day. Elyse entered his mind. His perfect ten. He imagined her blowing smoke rings. Then again he had never seen her smoke, didn't think she did. Such fantasy, like Bo. The record had spiralled to its core and began jumping. He lifted the diamond and let it play back from the beginning, crawling like fingertips on delicate skin.

He flipped on another record. Young Lust[40]. Here was a companion who knew how he felt, how he was, what he needed. *Only a dirty girl will probably have me*. He thought. But not dirty like Delilah. Something more perfect. Something for him. There could be purity in something dirty, after all dirt was the salt of the earth wasn't it? *Ah yes, salt*. He'd read girls tasted like salt down there in the pink parts. He could feel the saliva pool under his tongue. The song shifted to the next track and just as quickly shifted his mood, killing the sensations growing in his groin until he felt numb.

Maybe that was the answer, to lie still and submit to one's fate, as a hopeless nobody, that nobody knew nor cared for. Living a life within an empty room. Would that be so

---

[40] Gilmour, David & Waters, Roger. "Young Lust" from the album *The Wall*. Performed by Pink Floyd. Harvest/EMI & Columbia/CBS Records. 1979

bad? If he could clear the space of all its debris then nothing would be left. Nothing never felt so good. *Such a fool to trick myself.* It just reminded him that everyone was over there somewhere else. *Yeah, well I can be somewhere else too* he beat back into the pit.

He turned his head. His study books were still sitting open upon his desk where he had left them. The books that he'd been told were going to get him places. He wanted to believe it was true, after all that is what had been asserted to him. He dragged himself off his bed with the weighty pressure of his blood that dropped to the floor as he stood. He picked up his pen and turned to the next page trying to concentrate and commit to finish what he had started.

CHAPTER THIRTY-SIX

For the soft white tresses of an angel's main, Christmases had never looked so black, along with the days that scattered around it like tinsel that had lost its sheen through its ostentatious overuse. Trying to sunny up the side of the egg that cracked inside of the womb. Or more like the jar of roasted nuts his grandfather had received for a gift. *This is insane.* Damien rambled off in his head at the feelings the evening brought.

They had all gathered together for Christmas Eve. It was supposed to be a gift for him that they all be together. Mother, children, grandparents. He'd fed his mother enough black looks and non-sequiturs during prescribed visits over the preceding year. This response was their form of an apology, *her* form, which only made him equate it as a necessary ritual for him to endure, a celebration for which he deeply believed he was not really worthy in being there. It didn't matter. He wished he wasn't there anyway, as his eyes glazed over everyone, harder than any crackling. Rory chatted chirpily and hung close to Cynthia's side. He watched as his mother gently touched the back of his shoulder. It didn't look like it was for any particular purpose. *Why did she do it then?* He wasn't a little boy anymore, his hair was neat, his shirt was tucked, *why touch him, he will be fine without it*, he persisted. *And why are you smiling Claudia? You shouldn't be smiling at all.*

He stood up hastily from the table. He couldn't sit there any longer. The velocity with which he moved disturbed the cutlery and a knife fell to the floor making a resounding clang. They looked up briefly.

"Sorry," he gently expelled. He picked up the knife and placed it back on the table. "I, um, I am just going to get another drink." He picked up his glass and walked out.

How do I get out of here never to return? He went into his room and pulled out a cigarette from a half empty packet tucked at the back of his drawer, peeked down the hall to check no-one was looking before sliding onto the back veranda. He ducked behind the clematis vine, its flowers lost by the cold, lit the cigarette and breathed out into the icy cold night. Here he could see the red ring each time he breathed in and be just like his father before him. But here they couldn't see him to be able to recognise any reflection. Here he was hidden, well away from them. He felt like a black sheep dog chained in his cage in the snow that couldn't get out. Only another man can let an animal out of his cage. Unless there was some other supersonic force of nature that could do it.

It was so dark where he lived. The night was totally black in winter. Snow's white refracted. Or maybe just reflecting the space above. Out there, up there, maybe there was a hole he could disappear into. But if he were to be pulled into a black hole from where he was standing, everything else around him would follow him into it, never to come out. He didn't want anyone else to follow him there. He would have to find a way to get close enough to the tip of its accretion disk. Without a companion he could go it alone. Its inward spiral could consume him. And it was a one-way ticket. He was ok with that. And given no-one knows the answer to what is inside it, maybe he would end up in a parallel universe, where there was a copy of himself he could find and alter the course of his future, leaving this illusory universe with its phantom pain behind. There could well be another version of himself out there, the light just hadn't had time to reach him yet in order to see.[41]

He stubbed out the butt like a squished bug and quickly turned to head back inside. No use in pondering where his end of a star was. A loose piece of wire from the vine's lattice snagged him nicking the top of his shin and stuck a pleasant stinging sensation with a wasp-like bite. He looked down, pulling up the cuff of his pants and rolled down his sock. In the scratches of light coming through the door, he could see the red razor cut like a fine tear, where tiny droplets of pearlescent burgundy bubbled from beneath the skin. He put his finger on the wound lapping up the blood like a tongue. As he held his finger aloft, he had an urge to taste its forbidden wine. Like a stone is to a talisman, blood is to a life. His life. His life was bleeding all over the floor. He went inside and found a Band Aid® in the bathroom, brushed his teeth then changed his sweater. He decided to hide the wound, they didn't need to know. It didn't matter anymore.

He walked to the kitchen and poured a soda. Pots piled in the sink slurped with water the colour from a trough and an empty roast pan sticky with brown-black grease made him feel sick. All he could see was dead animal. The smell of fat on Formica®. He sipped on his soda, its citrus burst through the bubbles on his tongue. Its zest not strong enough to quell a

---

[41] Theories sourced from Chapter 6, Welcome To The Multiverse. Tegmark, Max. *Our Mathematical Universe*. 2014. First Edition. Alfred A Knopf. 2014.

silent night. He wanted to stay and wait in here and not go back to the table. The table where he'd talk through a forced conversation pretending to be interested in what was being said. He crinkled the bottle as he picked it up, its plastic crack split through the room. Civil obedience forced him back.

Cynthia nervously eyed him as he sat down.

"Well, Sylvia's boy has gone on to an Ivy League University. Scholarship. Isn't that impressive?" Claudia announced as she passed around the bowl of peas. It was the notable nod of her head that said it all, the way she extended it then tucked in her chin rippling the skin underneath.

"An Ivy Leaguer in this town." Cynthia demurely smiled.

"What is he studying?" Frank interjected.

"English I think." Claudia noted.

"Hm. What job does that get you?" He turned to Damien. "Do something that will get you a job."

Damien looked up feigning interest, then looked back at his plate, picking at the meat with his fork.

"Well I think he wants to get into academic teaching Frank." She eyed him across the room.

"That won't make him any money." He countered to Claudia.

"Learning is a wealth, whatever you do." She responded.

"As long as it's something." Cynthia gently offered.

"That's right. Something is better than nothing." Claudia relented. She picked up the bowl of peas from Frank and offered it in Damien's direction. "You want some more?"

He waved it away. His plate was fully piled with them. He hated peas. Like the conversation, one he had kept hearing so many times before, as numerous as the small green droppings on his plate. Such repetition.

"I'm going to be a pilot." Rory expelled between them.

"Oh is that so." Claudia exuded.

Crop duster, Damien chided. He stared at the food encrusted plates encircling the ornamental paper flowers that were perched in a tiny vase in the centre, beside the salt and pepper, like a fairy-tale protected by Jekyll and Hyde. He picked up his soda. The bubbles were starting to go flat, shaken by his loss of fervour, not that he had any at the start. He decided to fly the coop. He picked up his plate and collected Frank's which was cleaned of every skerrick and walked back to the kitchen. They brambled on behind him.

He looked out through the kitchen window, trying to find his event horizon. Didn't know why he was trying so hard looking for something you couldn't see. You are supposed to be able to see a horizon, why did they call it that then? Maybe that was the pun. It sucked you in, to nothing. Nothing but mind tricks.

CHAPTER THIRTY-SEVEN

'*Spring had brought him the hideous laugh of the idiot*'[42]. One that was a snide giggle and a dropped comment at the lockers that did it. "Nerd" he had called him. Test score results ranking Damien number one rendered such folly from a certain type of peer – from one in particular. He took to his pen in rapid fire return.

> *Rick, Rick*
> *Why do you have to be such a prick?*
> *Or maybe I should just call you a dick*
> *Oh Rick Dick*
> *You make me sick*

Elyse had overheard the snigger from Rick when she walked passed Damien as he was gathering books from his locker.

"Don't listen to him Damien," she had said to him.

---

[42] From Rimbaud, Arthur. *A Season in Hell. Selected Poems and Letters.* Translated by Jeremy Harding & John Sturrock 2004. London: Penguin Classics. 2004. Originally published as *Une Saison en Enfer*, France, 1873.

So very calmly and sweetly she had said it. He didn't know if he wanted to crumble in emasculated humiliation or sink to her feet in gratitude for her sympathy. Something dropped to the bottom of his heart, he wasn't sure what.

Damien may have been a nerd, but turds only came in one form – a shape of Rick. Damien penned the poem at the back of his exercise book as he tuned out the droll dictations of his teacher, and was soon propelled with a desire to tear out the page, roll it into a ball and flick it as a missile at the back of Rick's bulbous head. But there was Elyse, sitting behind his nemesis. He didn't want to hit her. In some sort of kismet, Elyse turned around briefly at that moment and caught his gaze and smiled at him. Maybe he should just fold it over and pass it to her, he thought. He wondered whether it would make her laugh. He turned the pages back to the middle, and turned to the teacher, catching the last of what he said.

Days came and days went. He caught up with the band for practise. It was the only sense of normalcy in his weeks. This is where he fit. Any lunch hour where he could escape away into the music room to be with them and play was a shining light and ignited a joy that everything else didn't. Any other time was a spine against cold concrete. If he spent too long there, it seeped into his organs freezing him to a sting-like burn.

Damien sat in the playground with his back against the wall. His view was its quadrangle. Girls, boys, unformed women, unformed men. They paraded themselves so normal, like everything was fine, that their lives ahead were as perfectly mapped as the paths behind them that they trod on their way passed him. *They can't help the way they are*, he thought to himself, for not knowing the shortness of the path they led to a life surrounded by a fence. A playing field he once wanted to be part of. He flipped open a spare page in his book.

I chuckle and stare at the fineness of view
A blister, a plague, confined here by you
Sally and Jessy and Bobby and Sue
Your liberty spell a knell in your tomb
Oh Elyse...

He was simply firing at sparrows again with his ink. He stopped and put his pen down. Elyse couldn't be part of the poem. Not this poem. He couldn't write about Elyse in this way. *Why can't you be mine?* He wanted to write. He avoided the yellow stain. He picked up his bag and headed away from the things burning his eyes. Home was better than here, just a different kind of heat.

Oh for Elyse. Elyse whom he glimpsed at from the corner of his eye as he sat two rows behind her to the side in class. He watched the plump curve of her breasts under her white blouse that had subtly started to pinch at the button making a pleat as time progressed, its cotton as soft as the skin he imagined that lay on its underside. Elyse who he caught in the hallway who always smiled at him and said hello and asked him how he was. Elyse who he could see at the other end of the playground waiting with her girlfriends for the afternoon bus, laughing baring her beautiful smile. If he caught her standing in the sun, her mousy auburn hair shimmered a honey golden blonde in its light. Elyse with the sweet smile bestowed upon him.

He pleasured himself to her picture, thinking about the strands of her honeyed hair, what it would be like to suck on its ends tapering from her neck where he traced a line round to her mouth. He wondered whether those lips tasted like the honey colour of her hair. Oh to taste those sweet lips. He yanked down hard until his hand became wet and a shooting propulsion jerked himself back. Elyse was the stuff of dreams. Elyse would never be his.

Elyse's smile was like the Crab Nebula's mariposa teasing its bull, awakening it back to life and hypnotising it into sleep. It enlivened an abundance of butterflies within him any time he was near her, then crashed like a crushed cocoon that was his reality. She was adoration unrequited. It was all a game – one that didn't always compute. Mi-Sex. Sex. No sex. He didn't care about Elyse anymore if she wasn't interested in him, yet he couldn't get her out of his head. He couldn't programme a girl to like him the way he wanted her to. Maybe he could just play with them. The way their smiles played with him. Or he could compose it into a song and play it as Dancing Demon[43] on the computer in the library. That's how he could make a girl dance for him.

He pumped out The Clash from his stereo. I'm Not Down.[44] He rattled the incantation over and over. It was only two more sleeps until he was going down – to the city - to see a concert. Hearing a band thrash was the surest way to remove himself from the dull flock. Their lack of interest in him was a social repellent in which he was eager to run in an opposing direction. The only way he was going to get there was under a cover of Patrick.

*

The theatre was packed, brimming with male sweat mixed with beer and second hand smoke of tobacco and hash. They both breathed in as hard as they could to suck in its sweetness. Patrick's brother was their senior companion, their ride in order to get into the city to see the band play. He

---

[43] Dancing Demon is a video game designed by Leo Christopher. 1979. Published by 80-NW Publishing. Powersoft Products. Radio Shack.

[44] Strummer, Joe & Jones, Mick. "I'm Not Down" from the album *London Calling*. Performed by The Clash. CBS/Epic. 1979

bought them both a beer at the start of the show. Its ginger ale barely covering its alcohol gave Damien a light headedness. In this environment it made him salivate for another.

The bass and drums pumped into the room and they banged their heads to each heavy thump. It was their ultimate rebellion as they bashed their bodies alongside their eager denizens, who yelled out with fists punched to the roof with each refrain. They were fire ants in the hole, leaping over each other's backs in angry revolution against the way it was on the outside. He didn't want to leave the nest, nor peak his head out for any air. This was the air he wanted to breathe.

The hot sweaty night stuck to their skin like a hooker's lick as they emerged from the theatre. They played more songs from their favourite bands loud in the cab of the car as Patrick's brother drove the way back home. They wound down the windows to let the wind rid the stench of beer and smoke from their clothes. They were like the sons of Vikings packed with the exhaustive grit of a return from their maiden voyage at sea, with a gait that accompanied it as they stepped out of the car. Patrick's house was dead silent when they walked in like escaped fawns finding their way home in a dark forest. Damien couldn't rid himself of the night's ecstasy as he tossed and turned in a sleeping bag on Patrick's bedroom floor. He relented to lie flat on his back and just stare up at the ceiling and imagine. He could taste the beer on his breath. It left a ginger fuzz and grogginess. He took himself back there. He wanted to relive it over and over.

Peter, Gary, Dean and Mandy didn't match the clash of symbols and aggressive guitar. There was more ordinance to the songs he played in the school band. Damien was starting to shrug ordinance. But he was at odds with the calm they brought him. He was the instrument he knew best – the pianoforte. Soft and hard. *Don't fight it. How do I combine the two?*

Don't fight it. How do I do what I want to do? Don't fight it! Don't fight it!
He ruminated in his head like a boxer going at it hard. He was
getting good at fighting though. Fighting with himself. Other
than in competition for a place, he never fought anyone else.
But he felt full of fight.

"Damien, can you come in here please?" Claudia
beckoned him from the kitchen two days later, as he walked
in after he arrived home from school. Her voice was brusque, a
sternness unusual for her.

"I spoke to Mrs Arncliffe today." She said mildly as she
pulled a pot out from the cupboard. Damien suddenly felt a
chill enter the room and a twist in his stomach.

"Oh yes," he responded apprehensively.

"She told me you boys went into the city on Saturday
night. You were drinking." She gazed across at Damien
disapprovingly. Damien didn't respond. He diverted his eyes.
"So is this true?" She persisted.

Damien looked up at her and raised his shoulders in
hunched defeat. His voice clogged in his throat. "Um." He
looked down at the floor.

Claudia shook her head disappointedly, as she rested her
hand on the bench. "I gave you money. You told me it was for
Mrs Arncliffe to pay for pizza. You lied to me Damien."

Damien continued to stare at the floor. He could feel
himself grow red in the face. She had never confronted him
like this before.

"It's no big deal." He looked away.

"What's that young man?" She gouged.

"Nothing." He stared back down at the floor in an act of
performance rather than in an act of caring.

"I hope you weren't spending it on funny cigarettes. I
know what they smell like you know." She looked at him
displeasingly, straightened her clothes then walked out.

You lied to me. You all lied to me. He wanted to say, as he felt a germinating anger mixed with despair. Claudia, his Claudia, who was his marigold, now with the eyes and voice of disappointment. *Why did you have to do this to Claudia?* He wanted to cry out to God. Not her. *Why are you doing this to me?* He obeyed the rules, did all the right things, he did everything he was told to do, everything he was bound by. A rope so constricted it left blistering marks around his wrists, the longer he was dragged by the cart. Carts were meant to carry people.

*

"I told you not to tell her! I told you not to tell her what we were doing!" Damien threw out rapidly with the venomous fisticuffs of his tongue. "You're meant to keep your mouth shut!"

Patrick stood there in the playground in front of him ashen as Damien spewed his words with viscous spittle.

"What am I to you? Huh?" Damien spat. Patrick took a step back. "Cat got your tongue?" He hissed.

"You're my friend." Patrick let out after a gulp of air.

"Yeah? Well you ruined it. You're no friend of mine. Get the hell away from me!" Damien swung his arm up into the air with a *vaffanculo* raise of his hand in vitriol.

"What?" Patrick looked on at him, feeling ashamed and confused. "I'm sorry. I didn't do it deliberately. She figured it out herself when she did the laundry."

"You ruined it. All of it. Don't come running back to me for anything!" Damien turned his head as he walked off angry. He didn't want to look at him.

Within the head he carried everywhere with him was an anger that was growing, expanding like sodium bicarbonate dropped into vinegar. A sour liquid that stung with a substance that muted, when combined exploded in paradox.

Soft and hard. *Don't fight it. Don't fight it. Don't fight it.* He rambled off in his head as he trod heavily out of the school yard, as though a starter's pistol had gone off. *Get away. I've got to get away. How do I get away from here?* You can run away from a gun, but you can't run away from hunger. It was a starvation borne from insides scooped out leaving him empty - desolate. The desolation raged at him, pounding like the hoofs of a bull, terrified of the things it knew was its enemy. Everything was a predator to him. Everyone. Trust was the predator. It was trust that tore. You can't stitch back an abstract notion – meta usurped its physics – a wonderful theory no longer testable. Only one theory remained tenable.

CHAPTER THIRTY-EIGHT

The end of summer burned as bright and hot as Venus, turning the leaves red, scorched by her temperament, or merely a transmission of his own.

Damien stood on stage at his keyboard as his band played through their chosen set. They were entrants in the region's battle of the bands. His town hosted the event in the oval where the field teamed with people from all the local towns. Fair stalls offered accoutrements and hoopla and a general vibration of fun soaked the air. The sun was hot in the sky as their songs jazzed through the afternoon. The crowd at the foot of the stage cheered and clapped as they finished their set. They had practised all summer. They were sure to win.

Mandy and Gary walked off the stage. Dean and Peter walked over to Damien on his keyboard and helped him shift the stand into the centre. This was consolation for the undying effort he had put into their sessions. His own solo piece. Peter gave him the thumbs up. Now he had fervour.

It was something he had written by himself and was nothing like what the band usually played. It was experimental, not only for him, but for the ears who were to drink it up.

He hit the beats, let his fingers grace the keys, his nerves held at bay. A bunch of people up the front nodded in time to the beat and a group of girls danced to the side. His heart flapped at the view. Two minutes later his eyes caught the sight of the ones who started to leave. A check shirt shook his head and waved a "not for me" gesture as he walked off. He watched as the crowd became a few people, gradually dispersing as he played, turning their backs with disinterest making their way toward the hot dog stands. Minced meat.

"It was cool. I liked it." Mandy had said to him as they packed up. Her words were better than no words he told himself. Then again he would have preferred silence in order to abandon the thing that failed.

"Yeah," he let out a half huff. "They just don't get it." He avoided her eyes.

His teacher gave him a ride home and dropped him at the gate. His bag was heavy and made his shoulder ache. The damp underfoot weighed him down like walking through mud.

When he walked into his room, he slammed the door behind him, dumping his bag with a force that tipped all his sheet music out scattering it across the floor.

"Fuck it!" He leaned down and shoved the sheets haphazardly back into the bag.

"Well aren't you in a fine mood," Ava penetrated into the space that had suddenly grown hot.

He looked up at her with a sniggering sideways glare.

"You shouldn't let things get to you." She feebly suggested, with a tiptoed unsureness in her breath.

"Tell it to someone who cares." He cut back tersely, uninterested in her suggestion.

Ava was taken aback. "Only losers go to fairs anyway." She flung her hand at him like a splayed deck of cards. A useless attempt to placate.

"Don't spit on me with your opinions you cunt." He condemned.

Ava double backed and stared at him gob smacked. She took a breath. "*This* gets you no-where." She hissed out with a scornful lick.

"You think you know everything. Ha! You know nothing! You are an infant! An insect! Such a little fool you are. You are no-one!" He spat out at her with a hyperbole ripped from its axis leaving a chartreuse stain.

"Why did you say that for? I never said anything like that to you!" She looked at him incredulously. "Why are you so angry?"

"Why are you so angry?" He mimicked back in a high pitched lambast.

She glared at him in the face. He couldn't look at her. Ava crawling around his temporal lobe left him with an itch too impenetrable. He felt a compulsive urge to launch himself upon her fuelled by a toxic desire to self-implode. He rushed out the door slamming it in her face as she dashed at him upon his exit.

He held the handle tight in his grip on the other side, pulling the door with a strength as oppressive as though he were pressing all his weight against it. He could hear her flagellate against it like a rabid animal, muffled flesh on bone, as she thrashed and pounded and bashed with her arms and fists screaming.

"Damien! Let me out!" She growled.

The only beat became silence.

He leaned against the door, resting his ear on its timber, where he could hear the sound of her stifled sobs. He opened the door and looked inside the room.

There in its centre was a girl, transformed, to the girl he

first saw at the brook, a girl of six, collapsed like a white dwarf, crouched and crying a heap of wasted tears upon his floor. How had she gone from an adolescent to a girl of six in the space of seconds?

He wanted to punch a hole in the door in fury. A venom grasped at his throat like he wanted to choke. He spat it out.

"You know the difference between you and me: I am going to be someone. You are going to be nothing." He sneered.

He walked out, slamming the door so hard it bounced on its hinges swinging ajar. He was already out down the hall as it reverberated to its rest.

How had he gotten here? What was he doing with a little girl? Why should he feel guilt for his rage? Ava and her questions. Questions he couldn't answer. Questions he couldn't fulfil. It was God that got angry. The God that made him. She was an albatross with its neck mistakenly limpid, taut around his, dragging him back down to the age of innocence. A relation as bent as the bough of a tree by the brook. Pulling him back down to when tears fell, where you cried when you were hurt. Damien didn't cry anymore. Tears were a waste. Their effluent waters a degenerative swamp clouded with its salt, no longer the crystalline sea they once used to be.

If he could have touched the face of a girl, any girl, to wipe away her tears he would have. It was a construct for which he never knew because he had never touched a girl, nor had there been any girl who had touched him. Getting that close was a fallacy, a faux representation. He didn't care if he couldn't get close enough to touch *her*. *I don't care*. He ultimately mused.

He could feel himself changing, but he couldn't see it. He wasn't the way he was before, but then again was he anyone before anyway? He didn't care about anything. He didn't care about anyone. *Why should I? I do things for me. Nobody else does.* It satisfied him that he should care for nothing at all. The change in his feelings was of them dropping away, along with his sight. He was the nocturnal bat, blind in the dark of a life that was getting too speckled with the swarm of insects in the distance or the transmission not reaching its channel muddying up the picture on the screen. But he had a picture he wanted to be in and he wasn't going to let anyone bar him from it. Not her, not anyone.

CHAPTER THIRTY-NINE

"...a world gone soft."[45] Damien laughed to himself as he repeated the line from The Men Who Make The Music. At least a couple of Devo's were making him laugh with the same degree of cynicism he'd started to acquire. Nobody else was. He scrambled to his console and switched to running Zork[46]. Its beauty was that its inbuilt play had a respondent on the other side. It was all coding, but it was like someone else was there with him in the room. Its script appearing on the screen he imagined as another human being on the other end of the line, talking to him. It distracted him from the false positive that was the singularity of each day alone, this day alone.

Mazes were made to get lost in. That was their purpose. Their makers always had to have a bounty to entice a player's entry, just as their makers had cut away an exit to enable their own escape. It was the view from the top that made it commanding and showed the brilliance of its grid. But it was the experience from within that captured the beating heart of

---

[45] From *Devo: The Men Who Make The Music*. Video by Devo. 1979. Reprinted with permission.

[46] Zork® is a computer game. (Anderson, Blank, Lebling, Daniels). Personal Software Infocom. 1977.

its prey – those who curiously stepped in. Damien always made it out alive. He had made it through in the Wizard of Frobox[47] to open the secret door at its end. But it was no end at the bottom of its endless stair. The disorientation after its exit, if it didn't make him stumble and trip, passed to reveal a new frontier. He could only imagine what that was.

He turned off the game. Today was going to be a good day he told himself. The down of his youth had started to grow as a bristling fur upon his chin and lip. He decided to shave. He wanted to be fresh and clean. All he did was nick a pimple and make himself bleed. Tissues stopped the blood at the gates.

He put on a clean t-shirt and jeans and brushed his hair. He looked at himself in the mirror. *It will do.*

Today was his birthday. He mounted his bike and rode into town. Claudia and Frank had given him money as a gift that morning before they left for church. Sixteen was an age where he was the best authority on how money should be spent on himself. Today he was going to buy a new games cartridge he had his heart set on and a music magazine from the local news agency which he had ordered. When he arrived at the store he was in luck, as his order had arrived. Its glossy ink made his eyes light up with anticipation and eagerness to get home and read it from cover to back. He handed over the cash in exchange for his prized goods, along with a packet of sherbet to keep in his back pocket for the ride home. Its tang always tickled his senses to the verge of a sneeze giving him a pleasant feeling of a happy reminder.

On the way back to his bike, he stopped into the coffee shop to buy a soda and a sugar doughnut to take back home as treats. As he walked in he thought he saw Frank's head in one of the booths. He cagily peered across and there he saw

---

[47] Zork® II: The Wizard of Frobox is a computer game. (Anderson, Blank, Lebling, Daniels). Personal Software Infocom. 1981.

Cynthia sitting opposite with Rory wedged in beside her – opposite a man who was indeed his grandfather – and Claudia on the other side. He wondered what they were doing here. Didn't know they were going to be here. He stopped still, contemplating whether he should walk up to them or not. A light flutter entered his heart *maybe they are here to surprise me*, he thought. But he wasn't sure. He hadn't told anyone he was coming into town.

He stood there and watched, obscured out of their line of sight behind a row of potted palms in the vestibule. Music was playing over a radio in the corner. Kim Wilde. He recognised it the longer he stood there with it worming its way into his ear. Frank stood up and with a wave to Cynthia; his heart panged and leapt in a somersault. He could see cups left in their places. His gut felt suddenly empty. Damien turned and fled from the shop as his grandfather headed to the door. He raced round to the laneway that ran down the side, as though in escape from a place he was forbidden to be. He felt overwhelmed. His heart pounded till it depleted and gave him a pain in the chest.

They didn't ask me to come. Why?

He walked back to his bike and lugged his legs on the pedals, with a weight commensurate with how he felt, like the day all the balloons at the fair had deflated and sunk in on themselves, only now more tormented and confounded as to why he should care. The feelings should subside not grow deeper. He wasn't a little boy who should care, but the trace of pain in his chest only seemed to dig deeper. He was bigger, his lungs were bigger, therefore there was more to deflate. His face dropped into a pallor as the wind brushed his cheeks. His body drained of all its essence, hollow, like it wasn't there. He pedalled harder to pump his blood, to get his body back. He pedalled faster and faster until he tore down the road in a rage that flushed his cheeks to burning hot, riding all the way to the creek until he ran out of breath, expiring with the heat. He wanted to scream.

He threw his bike to the ground and ran straight into the underside of the pines to the water's edge. In the darkness hidden from sun, shadows made out shapes – shape shifters, creatures and beasts curling the crook of their arms in the dark readying to crick his neck. His ears became acute to a thousand crawling insects that beat and chirped their way inside his head until it went wild with the coda: "da da da da da da da da da da da da da da…" It ruminated and pulsated ferociously as a hundred cackling hyenas. Its drum kicked and pummelled. He closed his eyes. He hoped it away. He placed his hands to his ears. He dipped his head down to bang the beat out when he lost balance and skidded his foot on the moss underfoot and slipped falling like a ball collapsed into the water hole, bashing the back of his ribs and scraping his arm on the boulder as he fell in. He sunk underneath its surface howling a tormented scream. He could feel the sting on his arm as it bled through the iciness, then shrieked as he burst his head skyward through the aqueous skin meeting the air, spent and out of breath, like a leopard who had run as fast as he could. He couldn't outrun its trailing black panther any more. He panted as his lips kissed the surface, with water drops spread like tears on his face. He wasn't sure if they were mixed with tears. He didn't know if he was crying. If *this* was crying. He gnashed his teeth in pain and cold that wrung a tight strain deep in his throat, like a current punched out from his jaw. He let out a cry of hoarse breath, until he finally caught it back, shivering through clenched teeth.

*

A pile of sodden clothes lay dumped in the laundry hamper. He lifted his clean dry shirt up in front of the mirror. The place where he struck the rock on his ribs was a red on-the-turn to a bruise like the head of a purple cauliflower. He touched it tenderly with his fingers. It stung.

The front door keys rattled as he walked swiftly back into the hall headed for his room.

"Why is your hair all wet?" Claudia asked with surprise when she saw him as she walked in the house.

"It's nothing." He quietly responded. Claudia tightened her lips at him, used to his aloof replies.

"You should have come to church this morning. Your mother came especially. She thought you would have been there."

Damien looked up with a mix of confused grief, disappointment, relief. It rendered a detached spatiality. He didn't say anything, just shrugged his shoulders. It was spilt milk. The collision with the rock had shattered it out of him.

"Never mind. She will be here later this afternoon. So make sure you don't go disappearing." Claudia stated it with a sad recompense, touching him on his shoulder as she walked into the living room.

Dark matter pulls things together. Dark energy pulls things apart.[48] In balance they made life. When the scales were tipped they rendered a cataclysmic disintegration of being that equalled the catastrophe of his heart. He felt its explosion akin to its release of internal energy. Yet he felt like collapsing in upon himself. He didn't know which way the lever was going. He wanted the complete annihilation of both extremes. To be rendered nothing. But the complete annihilation of matter only turned into radiation. He couldn't render nothing. Everything turned into something else. But that *something* was already empty. Nothing made sense. He just wanted to rid the emptiness from within him.

---

[48] Theories sourced from Chapter 6, Welcome To The Multiverse. Tegmark, Max. *Our Mathematical Universe*. 2014. First Edition. Alfred A Knopf. 2014.

Something to render him different.[49] As a particle in space he just needed to smash into something in order to feel.

He sat in his room waiting, like an embryo in the house of the rising sun[50]. Except the beams of its mandala were pointing inward like blades that stung with their flame instead of reaching their arms to some far off place lighting a different way. Dark energy was becoming too dense in danger of leaving him stillborn[51]. The only way he could live was to pack up and run. He knew he could still run. Then he could tell God he'd won.

---

[49] From Chapter Four: Relativistic Energy and Momentum. Feynman, Richard P. *Six Not So Easy Pieces*, copyright © 2001. Reprinted by permission of Basic Books, an imprint of Hachette Book Group, Inc.

[50] *The House of The Rising Sun* from the album The Animals. Performed by The Animals. Traditional folksong, arranged by Alan Price. Columbia UK/MGM US. 1964.

[51] Theories sourced from Chapter 6, Welcome To The Multiverse. Tegmark, Max. *Our Mathematical Universe*. 2014. First Edition. Alfred A Knopf. 2014..

Epilogue

A piece of himself tumbled like an acorn falling from its tree. He rested against its bark, as he sat looking out from underneath its canopy. He thought he saw Ava off in the distance. She looked like she was collecting acorns, underneath the base of an oak. Maybe she was going to walk over to him and show him all the pieces she had collected cupped in the palms of her hands. But she was too far away for him to see what she was doing. Then again, maybe it was just a mirage, because when he looked again she wasn't there.

The earth was round, apparently. Well, that is at least what he was taught. But from where he sat it was flat, with no curves at its edges, extending for miles with the same view far off in the distance. Clusters of trees to the north, wind rattled tips of wheat west, crops of rye east. It was all the same as far as he could see. Maybe he could make out the curves better if he looked out over an ocean, he thought. He was a long way from any sea. He was a long way from anywhere. He could only close his eyes to imagine himself someplace else. But after the dark of an eyelid, his eyes opened to black.

City lights were nowhere on the horizon. They only existed on a screen. He wondered what it would be like to be up high in a skyscraper staring out at a million pretty lights, scattered like stardust in a black void. He thought he might like to go and live in the city. *Maybe there will be more people like me*. But the thought of the city scared him, as much as its dazzle enticed. Maybe those lights were warning signs, like the ones at a railway crossing – if you didn't understand what they meant you could die.

The connections to this place were severing. He didn't belong. But he didn't know where he was meant to go. It was like an invisible hand pummeling his head and his chest producing a shocking sickness. A remorse for good and bad times past, like sobbing at the death of Piggy[52].

He watched up ahead in the distance to under the oak. Ava still wasn't there. Where did she go?

His room was loud inside the house. He was attached to everything in there yet was willing to leave everything behind. '*Frowning at the memory of so many destinies[53]*'. Posters of his heroes adorned the walls, boyhood toys remained on his sill, a keyboard rested underneath his bed that was spread with the same quilt he had from when he was six. It was the soul of the house. But the room looked too clean for a soul that was bleeding.

Cleaning out the old shoebox from under his desk, he found the old empty tin of chocolates still residing within it. He opened it up and hovered his nose over the top to find no scent remained. He tried to remember what the scent was, it had been so long ago. Something bitter sweet. He replaced it back in the box and decided to keep the rest of the things in there and put it back under his desk.

The sound of her voice he would never miss. That along

---

[52] Ralph cries over the death of Piggy, representing an act of remorse and an end to innocence. From Golding, William. *Lord of the Flies* First edition. 1954. Faber and Faber.

[53] From The Poet and the Muse. Verlaine, Paul. *Paul Verlaine Selected Poems* Translated by Martin Sorrell. First Edition 1999. Oxford University Press. 2009.

with the sight of her. She had brushed the hair on his forehead out of his eyes once, but the way she smelt and how she felt to touch was a memory that did not exist within him. It didn't matter. Nothing mattered anymore, other than the taste of the success he would show them. And he *would* show them. He was willing to take the risk for the life out there ‐ somewhere.

To dance upon the headstones of this life that he would bury was to be his valedictory. It was just sediment underneath, 'matter that settles to the bottom of a liquid'[54]. He would be able to float to its surface. He knew how he could be buoyant, what would take him there.

This life was like the spiral of a snail, circling downward. A shell to be crushed along with the slug that carried it. To crush was the only way to exit the vicious cycle, spiked with the spokes of a wheel. 'But already my desire and my will were being turned like a wheel, all at one speed.'[55]

I wish I could show you how I could love.

---

[54] Definition of "sediment". Australian Pocket Oxford Dictionary. 1976. Edited by Dr Bruce Moore. 6th Edition. Oxford University Press. 2007

[55] From Verse 142, Canto XXXIII, Paradiso. Dante Alighieri *The Divine Comedy*. Translated by Charles H Sission 1980. First Edition 1993. Oxford University Press. 2008

Acknowledgements

Literature

Frost, Robert. "The Door in the Dark" from West Running Brook. First edition 1928. Henry Holt & Co. 1928.

Hemingway, Ernest. Death In The Afternoon. 1932. First Edition. Vintage Classics, Random House UK. 2000.

Verne, Jules. The Chase of the Golden Meteor. 1909. First English Edition. Grant Richards, London. Sourced from Golia, Maria. Meteorite. 2016. Reaktion Books.

Feynman, Richard P. Six Not So Easy Pieces, copyright © 2001. Reprinted by permission of Basic Books, an imprint of Hachette Book Group, Inc.

Dostoyevsky, Fyodor. Notes from Underground. Translated by Jessie Coulson. First edition. 1972 London: Penguin Red Classic. 2006. First Published as Zapiski iz Podpolya, Russia, 1864.

Hinton, S.E. The Outsiders. 1967. First Edition. The Viking Press. Published in Penguin Classics 2007.

Shakespeare, William. The Tempest. 1610-11.

Shakespeare, William S. Sonnet 140. Public Domain. Sourced from database at www.opensourceshakespeare.org George Mason University Copyright © 2003-2022.

Baudelaire, Charles. A Voyage to Cythera; The Flowers of Evil. Translated by James McGowan. Copyright © 1993. First Edition. Oxford University Press. 1993.   First published as Fleurs du mal, France, 1857. Reproduced with permission of the Licensor through PLSclear.

Welcome To The Multiverse. Tegmark, Max. Our Mathematical Universe. 2014. First Edition. Alfred A Knopf. 2014.

Rimbaud, Arthur. A Season in Hell: Selected Poems and Letters. (Translated by Jeremy Harding & John Sturrock). 2004. London: Penguin Classics. 2004. Originally published as Une Saison en Enfer, France, 1873.

Golding, William. Lord of the Flies. First edition. 1954. Faber and Faber.

Verlaine, Paul. The Poet and the Muse. Paul Verlaine Selected Poems Translated by Martin Sorrell. Copyright © 1999. First Edition 1999. Oxford University Press. 2009. Reproduced with permission of the Licensor through PLSclear.

Australian Pocket Oxford Dictionary. 1976. Edited by Dr Bruce Moore. 6th Edition. Oxford University Press. 2007.

Dante Alighieri. The Divine Comedy. Translated by Charles H Sission 1980. First Edition 1993. Oxford University Press. 2008.

Popular Electronics Magazine. Ziff Davis Publishing Company. 1954-1982.

Musician Magazine. (Holdsworth & Baird). 1976-1981.

Montgomery, L.M. Anne of Green Gables. 1908. L.C. Page & Co.

Meares, Russell. The Metaphor of Play: Origin and breakdown of personal being. Third Edition. Routledge. 2005

Melton Knocke , Melanie. From Blue Moons to Black Holes. Prometheus. 2005

Tayler, R.J. The Stars: Their Structure and Evolution. 2nd Edition. Cambridge University Press. 1994.

Carroll, Lewis. Alice's Adventures in Wonderland. 1865. "The door between us" Public domain.

Ono, Yoko. Acorn. 2013. Algoquin books of Chapel Hill. 2013

Music

Miller, Glenn. Moonlight Serenade. Bluebird. 1939

Bowie, David. "Starman" from The Rise and Fall of Ziggy Stardust and the Spiders from Mars. Performed by David Bowie. RCA Records. 1972.

Nelson, Willie. "Bloody Mary Morning" from Phases and Stages. Performed by Willie Nelson. Atlantic. 1974.

Album by Pink Floyd. The Dark Side of the Moon. Performed by Pink Floyd. Harvest Records UK/ Capitol US. 1973.

Gershwin, George. "Summertime" from Porgy and Bess. 1935

Gibb, Barry & Gibb, Robin & Gibb, Maurice. "You Should Be Dancing" from the album Children of the World. Performed by The Bee Gees. RSO. 1976.

Felder, Don & Henley, Don & Frey, Glenn. "Hotel California" from the album Hotel California. Performed by The Eagles. Asylum. 1977.

May, Brian. Song "We Will Rock You". From album News of The World. Performed by Queen. EMI UK. 1977.

Hütter, Ralf & Bartos, Karl & Schneider, Florian & Schult, Emil. "Neon Lights" from the album The Man-Machine. Performed by Kraftwerk. Kling Klang / EMI Electrola. 1978.

Hütter, Ralf & Bartos, Karl. "The Man-Machine" from the album The Man-Machine. Performed by Kraftwerk. Kling Klang / EMI Electrola. 1978.

Hütter, Ralf & Bartos, Karl & Schneider, Florian. "Metropolis" from the album The Man-Machine. Performed by Kraftwerk. Kling Klang / EMI Electrola. 1978

Wonder, Stevie. "Superstition" from the album Talking Book. Motown. 1972.

Waller, Thomas "Fats" & Razaf, Andy & Brooks, Harry. "Ain't Misbehavin" from Connie's Hot Chocolates. 1929.

Gilmour, David & Waters, Roger. "Young Lust" from the album The Wall. Performed by Pink Floyd. Harvest/EMI & Columbia/CBS Records. 1979

Strummer, Joe & Jones, Mick. "I'm Not Down" from the album London Calling. Performed by The Clash. CBS/Epic. 1979

"The House of The Rising Sun" from the album The Animals. Performed by The Animals. Traditional folksong, arranged by Alan Price. Columbia UK/MGM US. 1964.

Wilde, Marty & Wilde, Ricky. "Kids In America" from the album Kim Wilde. Performed by Kim Wilde. RAK. 1981.

The Byrds: Untitled. Columbia. 1970

Bach, J.S. Minuet in G

Bach, J.S. Prelude in C Major

Television & Film

Steve Austin is the central character of the television series The Six Million Dollar Man. Reference is to the opening dialogue from Population: Zero, The Six Million Dollar Man. Season 1, Episode 1. Silverton Productions, in association with Universal Television. 1974

Alien. Brandywine Productions. Twentieth Century Fox. 1979.

Devo: The Men Who Make The Music. Video by Devo. 1979.

The Midnight Special. Burt Sugarman Productions. NBC Studios. 1972-1981.

I Dream of Jeannie. Sidney Sheldon Productions & Screen Gems & Sony Pictures Television. 1965-1970

American Bandstand. Dick Clark Productions & WPVI-TV & ABC. 1964-1981

The Partridge Family. Screen Gems Television & Columbia Pictures Television. 1970-1974

Josie and the Pussycats. Hanna-Barbera Productions. 1970-1972.

Godzilla. Toho Co Ltd. 1954.

Gaming & Electronics

Zork® & Zork® II: The Wizard of Frobox. (Anderson, Blank, Lebling, Daniels). Personal Software Infocom. 1977-1981.

TRS-80® is a computer manufactured by the Tandy Corporation. 1977.

Atari® is a video game console. Atari, Inc. 1972-1984.

Tank arcade game. Kee Games, Atari, Inc. (Bristow, Rains). 1974.

Death Race arcade game. Exidy. 1976.

Space Invaders arcade game. (Nishikado). Taito. 1978.

Dancing Demon. (Christopher). 80-NW Publishing, Powersoft Products, Radio Shack. 1979

Trademarks

Zork® is a registered trademark of Infocom, Inc.

Amor All® is a registered trademark of Energizer Auto & The Armor All / STP Products Company.

Mr Coffee® is a registered trademark of Newell Brands.

G Schirmer® is a registered trademark of G. Schirmer, Inc.

Cheetos® is a registered trademark of Frito-lay North America, Inc.

Mellotron® is a registered trademark of Markus Resch.

Coke® is a registered trademark of the Coca-Cola Company.

TRS-80® is a registered trademark of the Tandy AST Samsung.

Popular Electronics® is a registered trademark of John August Media, LLC.

Cocoa Puffs® is a registered trademark of General Mills IP Holdings II, LLC.

Smacks®is a registered trademark of Kellogg North America Company.

Roland® is a registered trademark of the Roland Corporation.

Yamaha® is a registered trademark of the Yamaha Corporation.

Ivory Soap® is a registered trademark of The Procter & Gamble Company.

www.ingramcontent.com/pod-product-compliance
Lightning Source LLC
Chambersburg PA
CBHW070014120726
47909CB00003B/929

* 9 7 8 0 6 4 5 6 7 4 1 2 5 *